BLACK CANDLE

THE SULLIVAN GRAY SERIES

H.P. BAYNE

BAYNE
INDEPENDENT
PUBLISHING

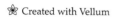

ACKNOWLEDGMENTS

A big thanks to my fantastic editor Hannah for helping me massage my manuscript into a book, and to Fiona Jayde for designing such a fantastic cover.

And the hugest thanks to my family and friends for all your support as I've set out to make my dreams of book publishing a reality. Whatever this journey brings, I'm grateful to have had all of you by my side.

1

THE RAIN STARTED LATE in the afternoon, moving from a drizzle to a shower to a full-out downpour in less than an hour.

From the dry safety of the Black Fox pub, Sullivan "Sully" Gray watched the unfolding scene, the front end of a prediction that tonight's storm was just the start of several days of weather bad enough to be dubbed "Biblical."

Kimotan Rapids—KR to those who called it home—was a city used to the rain, but that familiarity had its limits. This storm was expected to push everyone well past the point of comfort, bringing high winds, anticipated flooding and general carnage.

Here in the Riverview neighbourhood, the area's relatively safe position on the south bank was likely all anyone had to be grateful for today. At the Black Fox, where Sully worked as bartender, they'd expected a rush, given the anticipated need of shelter for those with few options. By five o'clock, they'd been proven right.

Sully's manager, Betty Schuster, sidled up to him and muttered in his ear. "What are the chances any of these people are actually going to buy a drink?"

Sully smiled. Betty had been a fixture at the Fox almost as long as it had been there—far longer than Sully's foster uncle, Lowell

Braddock, had owned the place. Betty knew the lay of the land and, while she grumbled about the struggling Riverview area and the Fox's regulars, Sully knew a good heart beat beneath the gruff exterior. She'd be fine with people sheltering in here as long as they behaved themselves and didn't try to steal or break anything.

Sully and Betty slung drinks for a while for those who had the money, offering water to the others. It was a few hours before a lull allowed for a quick break, and Sully headed to the back to get away from the crowd. Cracking the door to the rear parking area, he saw a police cruiser pull to a stop.

Sully watched as his older brother, Dez Braddock, unfolded his six-foot-six, muscular frame from the driver's seat and stretched the kinks out before trotting over and ducking through the door. Dez took a moment to brush the rain from his cropped red hair and the shoulders of his uniform before greeting Sully.

"Weather's a bitch, huh?"

"Doesn't look good."

Dez scoped the bar from the employee entrance, then returned to Sully. "Pretty packed house in there."

"People need a place to stay dry until the shelters open."

"Everyone behaving? No one's looking like they're going to get out of control?"

Sully quirked up a corner of his mouth, one eyebrow following suit. Dez's ploy was obvious, the consummate protector aiming to ensure Sully was okay and would stay that way.

"No one's really got the money to get out of control," Sully said. "A few people are drinking, but we don't sell it by the bottle. Not many people in there today are eager to dish out four bucks for a beer or five for the hard stuff."

Dez nodded, satisfied—for now, anyway. Sully had no doubt he'd be back to check in within a couple hours, as long as he didn't end up on a longer call.

"You working a night shift?" Sully asked.

"Swing, two to two."

"What about Eva?"

"She's on days right now, so at least I get to see her at night for a bit. Sometimes I think it would be nice if we were on the same shift, but I guess it's still working a little better this way for Kayleigh."

"How is she?"

Dez chuckled. "Terrible threes."

"I thought they stopped at two."

"Not with my kid. Mom said I was a real asshole at that age, so she figures I had it coming. You need to come over. She's always good with you."

"Mom, you mean? Yeah, she always liked me better."

Dez giggled and elbowed Sully. A guy his size giggling might have raised a few eyebrows, but not among those who knew him. Dez had the stature of a bear, but he was more teddy than grizzly —as long as you didn't cross the people he loved. A man as ready with his emotions as he was could also be quick to anger under the right circumstances. Thankfully, with Dez, those occasions were few and far between.

"What's the plan for tonight?" Sully asked. "If things get crazy out there, I mean?"

"Those of us on the swing shift could wind up with OT if things go sideways. If things go really bad, Eva's shift might be called back in, too, but that's a worst-case scenario."

"What counts as worst case?"

Dez shrugged. "We'll know it when we see it, I guess. But full evacuation of The Forks for starters. Gateway Dam overflowing would be taking things up another level yet. Fingers crossed it won't get as bad as they're predicting. "

Dez might have been the protective older brother, but he didn't corner the market on worry. "Be careful out there, D, okay? Don't do anything stupid."

Dez beamed down at Sully. "When have you ever known me to do anything stupid?" Sully raised his eyebrows, leading to another laugh from the larger male. "Yeah, okay, point taken, kiddo. I'll be careful. Promise."

Sully decided against arguing. It wouldn't get him anywhere, anyway. "You have time for a drink? I could get you a soda."

Dez checked his watch. "Ah, hell, why not? I've got nothing going at the moment."

Dez followed Sully into the bar where Sully pulled a cola for his brother and another for himself. With standing room only tonight, they hovered around the end of the bar, watching Betty's futile-yet-unending attempt to remove a stain from the bar's surface.

"I think it's part of the wood grain," Sully said. "But she won't listen. It drives her nuts."

Dez chuckled. "Probably my fault. That time I came in here to wash up after I had to pull that suspect out of the dumpster? I told her I put that stain there."

Sully grinned but gave Dez a shove anyway. "You're such a jerk."

Dez was readying to shove Sully back when his face registered recognition. "Bulldog! How's it hanging?"

Sully followed Dez's gaze to see Billy "Bulldog" Bird lumbering over, his face even limper than usual. Bulldog had earned his nickname thanks to a fine set of jowls and a temperament that ranged from loyal and friendly when sober to snarling and snapping when drunk. Bulldog, as far as Sully knew, slept in the park most nights along with numerous other homeless people, at least until temperatures started to drop in the fall. At that point, he and the others started clamouring for space at the shelters or searching for friends who would give up the use of their sofas for a few months. Bulldog had stayed with Sully a few times during the winter months when he'd been too drunk to safely make it anywhere else.

It was too early for Bulldog to be drunk; he liked to drink but it didn't rule his life, and he typically preferred to stay fully sober until the sun set. But a sober Bulldog was usually laughing and joking, and this Bulldog—the one coming toward them with deadened eyes and a miserable, drooping face—wasn't that guy.

"What's going on with you?" Dez asked.

"Not here, Copper. People are gonna think I'm a snitch."

"You are."

"Piss off."

Sully led the way into the back, pulling up a chair for Bulldog. A quick study of the man failed to reveal if he was depressed about something or if he was ill, as his face tended toward flushed at the best of times. Either way, it looked like he needed to sit down. They all knew it had been a rough few months for him, even by the high standards set by the street.

Dez leaned against the wall and regarded the older man. "Okay. We're alone. What's up?"

"I don't know, Copper. Things have been shitty lately. Just having a down day, I guess. I can't explain it."

But Sully could.

The back area was lit by a couple of dim bulbs that barely made a dent in the shadows lingering in the corners. Out of one, a woman emerged, long black hair and shadow obscuring much of her face, hands bound and held out before her, one cupped around the other. While he could make out little of her eyes, the way her head was angled made it clear her attention was on Bulldog.

She materialized at Bulldog's side and remained there, staring. Just staring. And now, the distance to her lessened, Sully recognized some of the shadow around her face and neck as something else. Bruises.

"Sully, what?"

Sully inhaled sharply, startled by his brother's question. "Huh?"

"What are you loo—" Dez broke off mid-question, his expression and his movements revealing he'd clued in. Dez was one of the handful of people who knew, and he'd safeguarded Sully's secret since childhood. Dez had been all about helping his new foster brother find his way in life back then; part of the master plan was ensuring no one knew Sully could see the dead.

It was a detail Dez was plenty happy to ignore where possible, terrified as he was by the mere thought of ghosts. Pity for him, because Sully's life had been filled with them.

Dez gave up his spot by the wall, approaching Sully and tugging at the smaller man's T-shirt to pull him toward the stairs, removing the two of them to a spot where conversation would remain private. Bulldog didn't so much as look up, his attention anywhere but on the brothers. But Sully had a hard time looking away as the spirit raised her arms and brought them down in a chopping motion against Bulldog's right shoulder. The assault would have knocked a man to the floor had the woman solid limbs to work with. Something registered nonetheless, and Bulldog reached up to rub lightly at the shoulder before dropping back into thought. The woman raised her arms again, this time higher and aiming for Bulldog's head.

"Stop it," Sully said. The woman's head snapped up, and Sully could make out one blackened, milky-white eye staring at him through a gap in the hair before she vanished.

Sully had at last succeeded in gaining Bulldog's attention. "Stop what?"

"Give us a second," Dez said, towing Sully a few more feet away. Then, "Where is it?"

"She's gone. For now, anyway."

Dez heaved a sigh that would have been comical had it not been for everything Sully had just seen.

"I think she'll be back, though."

Dez looked up sharply. "Where? Here?"

"If I say yes, you'll never come back, will you?"

Dez shifted from one foot to the other. "Of course I'd … Jesus, Sull. You know I hate this stuff."

"You know how I told you ghosts sometimes haunt people, not places?"

"That's why you end up with all the extras from 'Sixth Sense' hovering around you."

"A lot of them have found me because they think I can help.

But this one's not haunting *me*. I think she's hanging around Bulldog. It probably explains why he's been so depressed lately. They can impact people's moods and health without anyone knowing. Sometimes the stronger ones can even influence people's actions."

Dez paled behind his freckled tan. "So she's not hanging around you then?"

Sully quirked up the side of his mouth. As much as it bothered Dez to be anywhere on the same block with a ghost, he'd never backed down to the idea of one when Sully needed him. Sully had learned to tolerate his unwanted visitors over the years, but his childhood had been terrifying. After he'd been placed at age seven with the Braddocks, he'd spent many a night tucked up in bed next to his new foster brother while Dez, three years his senior, prattled on about whatever came to mind until Sully fell asleep. Judging by the bags under Dez's eyes in those days, he hadn't found sleep as quickly, and Sully imagined he'd spent another hour or two searching the lamp-lit room for invisible intruders. And yet Dez never complained, never once sent Sully back to his own room. He'd simply sucked back his own fear so he could help Sully through his.

"No, this one's not on me. She seems pretty fixated on Bulldog."

Dez's relief showed in the relaxing of facial muscles and the release of shoulders, but he didn't look a whole lot happier. "I hate to ask, but what does she look like?"

"Long, black hair, Indigenous, I think. Her hands were tied in front of her. The hair was in front of her face, so I couldn't make out much for features, but it looked like she had a black eye. And there were bruises around her neck, I'd say from hands."

"Like she was strangled," Dez said. A statement, not a question.

"You know her."

"Breanna Bird. She was Bulldog's younger sister. I'm not sure if you remember it from the news, but they found her body a month ago. Major Crimes didn't release many details publicly, but she was found pretty much exactly as you just described."

Dez leaned down, as if the hushed tone of their conversation was no longer enough.

"You only see them when someone's killed them, when they're after justice, right?" He didn't wait for the answer; he already knew it well. "We busted the guy who killed her. Breanna's common-law confessed. I mean, Danny hasn't been all the way through the courts yet, but he's charged and in custody, and the case is a pretty good one, I think. What do you think she'd be after?"

Given what Dez had said, Sully couldn't imagine. "No idea. But whatever it is, she seems pretty intent on getting it."

2

DEZ MANAGED to score himself a dinner break, allowing him to stay a bit longer at the bar.

And Betty had business well in hand, giving Dez, Sully and Bulldog some extra time to sort through Breanna's sudden appearance.

In all honesty, Dez would have liked to be anywhere else, ghosts right up there with contagious disease and ballet when listing the topics he least liked to discuss. But he was well enough versed in Sully's visions—or gift or curse or whatever it was—to know there had to be something to this. The Major Crimes unit had put this case to bed a couple of weeks ago, having moved on to a particularly disturbing home invasion that had left an elderly man dead. There were some loose ends to tie up on the Breanna Bird case, true, but the bulk of the investigation was complete.

That said, it was now quite possible there was more loose about the case than just a few wayward strands. It could be the whole thing was about to unravel.

Sully had pulled up a chair next to Bulldog, allowing them to speak quietly while Dez monitored from his spot along the wall. He liked to position himself somewhere he could watch Sully's eyes. If they fixed on something Dez couldn't see, he would know which area of the room to avoid. He'd never seen one of Sully's ghosts despite the knowledge he'd shared plenty of space with them over the years. He'd be happy to keep it that way.

Sully was working on easing Bulldog into this world gradually. "You've been feeling tired and sick for a while now, haven't you?"

Bulldog nodded slowly.

"Since your sister died?"

"Yeah, I think that's what started it. She was a good girl, you know? She had a big heart, always gave me a place to stay when I was in her neck of the woods. Hard to get past something like that happening to her."

"Grief's a bitch," Dez said. He knew grief. He'd carried it his whole life.

"Who'd you lose?"

Dez scuffed a boot across the floor, focused on its progress to avoid sinking too deeply into memory. "My brother Aiden. I was eight. He was just five."

"Jesus, that's the shits. What happened?"

Dez didn't want to go too far down that path. Not now. Not ever, come to that. "He drowned."

The two words took Dez back there anyway, standing in a funeral home, trying to rationalize how Aiden's whole body, small as it was, fit into that tiny urn. For months after, he'd looked for him, listened for his laughter, prayed he'd wake up and discover it was all a vivid nightmare. Instead, he was left with the unwavering reality he'd never be able to take back that final morning when he'd been too annoyed to play his little brother's game of hide and seek. Dez hadn't found him, hadn't even tried, not until it had become brutally obvious there was no longer anyone there to find.

Dez had gone to bed that first night to the sound of his mother's tears and the knowledge his father would be out all night with the search party Dez hadn't been allowed to join. He had prayed he'd wake up to see Aiden poking him awake as he often did, his impish smile prodding him into one annoying game or another. Instead, Dez had awoken to a godawful quiet, broken only the next day by his mother's screams as she was told they'd found Aiden dead along the banks of Kettle-Arm Creek. Ever since, Dez carried the knowledge Aiden had been down there because of him. Because he had been so frustrated with Aiden he'd momentarily wished him away.

There would be no waking from that reality, from the guilt and the pain it elicited. But he could at least find some peace in the here and now, which he'd been pulled back into by Sully's gentle pat on his leg. Sully remained visually focused on Bulldog, but he always had Dez somewhere in his sights.

Bulldog grunted mournfully, a sound Dez recognized as both empathetic and consoling. "Sorry, Copper."

Sully dove back in, steering the conversation away from Dez and his past. "The thing is, Bulldog, sometimes grief only explains so much. Sometimes there's more to the way people feel than what's inside them. Sometimes, it's also about what's outside."

Bulldog narrowed his eyes appraisingly. "Are you drunk, kid?"

"Do you ever feel like she's still around? Maybe you smell a perfume she liked or catch sight of something out the corner of your eye or hear someone calling your name when there's no one there."

"Are you asking me if I believe in ghosts?"

"I guess I am, yeah."

"Then, no. I don't. At least not the way you're suggesting. I was raised that people die, and they go to Heaven or Hell."

"So what about all the things people see?"

"Hallucination maybe. Or some sort of demon. I don't know. Hell, I don't even really believe in any of the Heaven and Hell stuff, come right down to it. If there's a God, where the hell's he been all my life? I sure don't see him rushing to help anyone I know."

"I don't know anything about God, but I do know about what happens after we die."

"How? You ever been dead?"

"No, but I've met plenty who are."

No matter how many times Dez heard Sully say the words, it still unnerved him, the chill running down his spine as he thought back to the various people his little brother had described over the years. Add to that the condition they'd been in at the time, and you were left with one hell of a living horror movie. No acting required.

Bulldog craned his neck to peer up at Dez. "He on the level here?"

Dez nodded slowly, trying for a smile that never really formed.

"And he's not crackers?" Bulldog asked.

"Sully? He's his own brand of quietly crazy, but not when it comes to this. He's telling the truth, man."

Bulldog's eyes snapped back to Sully's face. "So you're about to tell me my sister's haunting me, is that it?"

"I wasn't going to say it like that."

"Is there another way to say it?"

Sully shrugged. "Not really, I guess."

The chair hit the wall as Bulldog leapt off the seat and made for the back door. "This is nuts. I can't do this right now."

Dez took two quick strides and cut his friend off at the pass. "Just wait a second, okay? I know how this sounds, believe me. I didn't buy all this stuff either until I met Sully. But it's real. No one hates saying that more than me, but it's true. And when he sees stuff, it's for a reason. He only sees people who've died because of something someone else did to them, the ones who need justice."

"Bree got justice," Bulldog said. "Her stinkin' common law is in remand waiting trial for killing her. Danny's gonna rot in jail and then he's going to burn in Hell. Sure sounds like some sorta justice to me."

"Something's not right," Sully said. "I'm not saying they

didn't get the right man. I'm just saying something's not right. She knows it, and she needs you to know it too. She's been hanging around you for a reason, and she needs help."

"Yeah, with what? What could she possibly need help with? She's dead, man. Dead people don't need help. It's the people they leave behind who do."

"That's not always true," Sully said. "Sometimes they get stuck here, and they need help to get where they need to go."

"Well, I'll help *you* figure out where to go."

"Bulldog." The edge in Dez's voice turned the name into a warning. It wasn't easy for Sully, seeing the things he did and, on occasion, acting on them. While there wasn't much Dez could do to help out with the ghost side of things, he was happy to fall back on size, muscle and affection for his brother to look after Sully within the living, breathing world.

Bulldog knew that well and recognized the danger he was stepping into. Anyway, Bulldog liked Sully, and not just because he might give him a place to crash now and again.

"I'm sorry, Sully. I just don't want to talk about this, all right?"

Sully nodded and managed a small smile. "I'm here if you change your mind."

Bulldog didn't respond in words, just nodded. He was about to head out the rear door into the rainy alley when Sully stopped him with an offer.

"Why don't you stay here tonight? You can have the couch in my room."

Bulldog's face split into a toothy grin, turning him into a closer approximation of the man Dez had known in the days before Breanna's death.

"You're a peach, kid. Lot nicer than your oaf of a brother there." He turned and patted Sully on the cheek, reserving a solid jab for Dez's gut. Dez managed to shift his abs back a bit but still ended up doubled over in a coughing fit while Bulldog laughed it up.

"He's not going to be an easy customer on this," Dez said once

Bulldog had headed upstairs to Sully's one-bedroom apartment. "I'm not so sure he's got it in him to do anything about Breanna."

"I've seen her," Sully said. "I don't think she's going to give him much of a choice."

BY TEN THAT NIGHT, most of the crowd had left the bar, headed off to fight for space at the nearby shelters or, for those who had one, home to ensure the place hadn't yet flooded.

The rain fell harder, at times pouring down in sheets that made it impossible to see across the street. Sully had all but pushed Betty out the door, urging her to head home before things got worse. And, for what could easily have been the first time in her life, she hadn't argued.

Betty was nervous, that much was obvious. She'd seen severe storms in the past, but she'd become a broken record of doom tonight, proclaiming this as shaping up to be the worst by far.

It wasn't just raining anymore, lightning flashing alongside cracks of thunder and a wind alternating the rain's course between sheer vertical drop and full horizontal.

The power had been coming and going for the better part of an hour and it finally quit altogether, causing the bar to fall back on the generator. But that didn't help with everything, the oak-panelled interior left darker than usual and the till out of commission, leading to the final mass exodus of the night. Only two people remained in the bar: Sully and Edgar Maberly, a man somewhere in his seventies who'd been coming here pretty much since the Black Fox was established, and who seemed to pride himself on being the last one out every night. But, like most nights, Edgar wasn't much aware he'd won that particular contest, having passed out at his usual table in front of a half-finished glass of cheap scotch.

Sully was about to wake him and call a cab when his cellphone rang.

"Hey, Dez. How's it going out there?"

"Fine, long as I don't have to get out of the car. Unfortunately, with everyone stressed out and indoors, we've had three domestics already tonight, and it doesn't look like that's likely to change anytime soon. How's everything there? Your power out?"

"Yeah. Doubt it's coming back on tonight, either. I can't imagine they'd send crews out in this."

"No, we've been told crews are only going out on emergency calls. The public's been warned to get by on generator power or to do without until things calm down a bit. How's Bulldog?"

"I went to check in on him about an hour ago, and he was crashed out on my couch."

"So, in other words, he's fine. You? You get everyone out okay?"

"Just me and Eddie left in here."

"So a typical night then. And, uh … anything else?"

Sully smiled, let it show in his voice. "Any sign of Breanna, you mean."

"It's not funny. None of it is funny."

"No, it's not. But you are. Don't worry; if she's going to change tacks at any point, she'll come at me, not you."

"And that's supposed to make me feel better?"

"She's just a person without a body, Dez. That's all. A person who needs help."

"Yeah, whatever. Listen, I wanted to tell you, I made a call to a friend in Major Crimes. The lead investigator on the matter was Forbes Raynor. He's a real jerk, and his investigative technique leaves something to be desired, but my friend backed Raynor's play on this. Sounds like they really did get a confession from Danny. He didn't go down for it easy, but he did go down. Admitted to the whole thing. Of course, now that he's been appearing from time to time in front of a judge, he's singing a different tune, saying he didn't do it."

That was interesting. Given Breanna's presence, very interesting.

"Sully, you hear me?"

"Yeah. Just thinking."

"Wanna include me?"

"She seems pretty intense to me, even comparing to others I've seen. What if Danny didn't do it? What if the real killer's still out there?"

"He confessed, Sull."

"People confess to things they haven't done sometimes, don't they?"

"Sure, people with cognitive issues or brain injuries can sometimes be guided toward a confession. But Danny's neither. He can be a goof, but he's more or less in working order."

"Any idea how much detail he provided during his confession?"

Sully could hear Dez's frown through his reply. "Not much."

"Sorry?"

"I said, not much. He admitted to strangling her, though, and tying her hands."

That was something, Sully guessed. Danny would've had to be there to know those things. Even if he didn't physically do the deed, if he'd been standing idly by while someone else did, that was pretty much the same thing.

But, if that were the case, it meant someone else was out there.

"I know what you're thinking, Sully, and no. Danny acted alone. It was a domestic. He said he hit her, gave her a black eye. After that, things just went from bad to worse. I see it all the time. Abuse starts out small, builds over time. Eventually, it can end with someone dead."

Sully knew that was true. He'd lived in several foster homes before coming to the Braddocks, enough that he'd learned what abuse was, how it worked. He had the physical and psychological scars to prove it. They'd largely healed, thanks to time and an excellent child psychologist his foster mom Mara Braddock had taken him to. But while the marks had faded, they were there all the same and no doubt always would be.

But, as far as Sully could tell, this didn't begin and end with abuse. Not the way Breanna had been whaling away on Bulldog.

"You know, when you go all quiet like that, I can actually hear your gears turning, Sull. What's on your mind?"

"She wasn't just hovering around Bulldog. She was trying to hit him. Hard. Like she was trying to get his attention or ...."

Sully didn't bother finishing the statement. Dez would know what he'd left unsaid. "Bulldog doesn't have it in him, Sully. He's a good guy."

"When he's sober, sure. But I've seen him drunk. It's not pretty."

"He wouldn't have killed his own sister. No way in hell. Not even drunk."

"Yeah, you're probably right."

Dez was the one working the long silence now.

"Dez? You there?"

"Jesus H. Christ. You really slay my nerves, you know that? Why'd you have to invite him to stay if you suspected he might be a frickin' murderer?"

"I didn't say I suspected him. I'm just trying to look at all the possibilities here."

"Well, stop looking. You make me nervous. Is there somewhere else he can go just so I'm not up all night worrying about your ass?"

"He's got nowhere else to go. You know that."

"Yeah, well, much as I like the guy, he's not my problem. You are. I'll come get him, drive him around until I find him a bed somewhere, all right? Just hang tight with Edgar until I get there."

Sully was about to tell Dez it wasn't needed when he heard movement at the door leading from the bar to the employees' only area and spotted Bulldog there, slack-jawed and wide-eyed.

"Dez, gotta go. Bulldog just came down and he looks like ...."

Edgar announced his return to the waking world by adding his own overly loud two cents' worth. "Like he's seen a goddamned ghost."

3

Sully clicked the "end call" button, ignoring Dez's barked orders to the contrary.

"Bulldog, you okay?"

Bulldog shook his head no. "I think you need to have a look at something upstairs."

"Let me get Edgar a cab, and then I'll lock up and follow you."

"I don't think it's going to wait that long."

Considering his options, Sully decided to lock up with Edgar inside. But no way he was leaving the guy alone in the bar with the beer fridge sitting within easy reach; Edgar could have the contents half gone by the time Sully was done upstairs with Bulldog.

Sully turned the sign to "closed" and locked the front entrance, then returned to Edgar. "Come on, Eddie, time for a little walk."

"Don't need no friggin' walk. 'M fine."

"Yeah, I know you are, big man. You're taking me for a walk."

Edgar grunted, which Sully took as plan approval, and the older man allowed Sully to heave him out of his chair.

Bulldog was still standing at the door to the employee area, vibrating with anxiety as Sully looped one of Edgar's arms around his neck to keep the guy on his feet. The stairs were going to be a bitch, so Sully left Edgar sitting on the bottom step while he closed and locked the door that separated the back area from the bar. He grabbed a flashlight from the utility closet and followed Bulldog up the stairs.

"Where the hell you goin', kid?" Edgar slurred after them. "What about my walk?"

"In a minute, Eddie. Just sit tight."

Bulldog stalled at the partially ajar door to Sully's apartment—the only occupied suite of three up here—and refused to go any further.

"What's wrong?" Sully asked.

"I told you I didn't believe in ghosts, right? I might have been a little hasty."

"Why?"

"You'd better see for yourself."

"You coming?"

"Not on your life."

Sully took a deep breath and put a hand on the door, steeling himself to push it open. He'd been seeing ghosts as far back as he could remember, but it wasn't something he'd ever grown used to. Some people, he'd heard, were lucky and saw only the ones who had already crossed into the light. Others saw all manner of spirits. Sully just got the ones who had died violently, leaving his memory filled with blood, bruises, slashes, gunshot wounds, burns, horrific breaks, gore and virtually every other type of wound a person could imagine. They weren't pretty, they weren't at peace and they sure as hell didn't make sleeping an easy feat many nights. The sight of them didn't leave him traumatized as it once had, but there was still that creeping dread whenever he knew he was about to walk into a situation with one. There was the sense of the unknown, and there was past experience too. While many of the dead realized what had happened to them, some didn't, and some were still caught up in death throes. Terror, rage and confusion could turn people into caged animals willing to bite anyone who got too close, and the only difference between the living and the dead was the simple encasement of flesh, blood and bone. The dead could lash out too, and Sully had been on the receiving end more than once.

But there was no way to know what he was dealing with until he went in there.

Sully pushed open the door, finding his apartment encased in darkness as expected. The generators were taking care of a handful of lights in the rest of the building, but the backup power didn't extend to the apartments, which operated on their own power supply.

Sully clicked on the flashlight and stepped inside.

He'd never been able to hear them; his ability, for whatever reason, was restricted to sight, sense and sometimes smell. And yet, the first thing he was aware of was a sound.

There was nothing rhythmical about it, a series of light thuds and what sounded like flapping. A short hallway led past the bedroom and a bathroom and then into the combination kitchen and living room. The bedroom was quiet and the bathroom, too, leaving just the main room to contend with.

Sully took another big breath and released it quietly before forcing his feet forward.

He detected movement to his right and he ducked as something breezed past his head. He had dealt with poltergeists before, and they were never easy. They tended to be angry, powerful and stubborn—a miserable combination for anyone trying to help them.

But this felt different. The thing that came at him didn't seem like a hurled object so much as something alive, and his theory was backed up by the noise he continued to hear. And he knew now what it was.

He scanned the room with his flashlight, guided by the sound of the bird's flapping and thudding, and found it fluttering next to the window nearest the sofa. The windows were all closed, leaving Sully to question how it had managed to get inside. Not wanting to add to the creature's existing fear, Sully headed to the other window and reluctantly opened it, receiving an immediate response in the form of a blast of cold rain. With any luck, it would be enough to guide the bird out.

Unfortunately, it didn't take the hint, so Sully pulled the comforter from the couch and tried to get behind the bird, expecting the only option would be to catch it. He tried to shoo it toward the window but, while it flew in that direction, it didn't find the opening, instead hitting the wall with a thud. Sully dropped the comforter and used the flashlight to find the stunned bird on the floor.

He carefully picked up the small body—a brown sparrow from what he could tell—and decided it would do better if released downstairs. He didn't want to put a disoriented bird on the window ledge and risk it falling to the pavement a floor down.

He couldn't carry the bird as he was and pick up the flashlight, so he left the latter where it was and walked toward the strip of light showing in the hall from the landing outside. He had nearly convinced himself all that had scared Bulldog was the inexplicable presence of the little bird—now beginning to stir gently in his hands—as it flapped against the walls, seeking escape.

Then, the landing outside just a few steps away, the door slammed shut in his face.

He stopped dead in his tracks, sensing something—someone—behind him. From the opposite side, there was a pounding at the door, an ineffectual rattle of the handle, and he could hear Dez shouting his name.

Sully knew without even trying the door that Breanna wouldn't let him leave until she'd said what needed to be said.

Turning, he found her standing there as he knew he would, visible to him despite the lack of light. She stood a few feet away, face covered by the curtain of her hair, hands bound and reaching out in front of her.

Swallowing his fear, Sully had to try twice to form his question.

"What do you need me to see?"

She moved toward him so fast it was like a blink. Sully flinched but held his ground. He could see one of her eyes now, the blackened one, the surface distorted by the milky sheen of death. He had to force his eyes past that so he could study the hands she was now lifting toward his chest.

"Sully!" Dez shouted. "Open the damn door, man, or I'm gonna kick it in!"

"I'm okay," Sully responded, just loud enough Dez would hear. "Give me a minute."

Breanna hadn't moved, save her cupped hands, which were now slowly opening. Sully watched as a purple flower with a bright yellow centre, fully visible in the darkness, came into view.

Sully was no botanist, but he had a feeling he needed to get this right. "Is that lavender? A tulip? Orchid?"

She had yet to respond. He was failing miserably.

"Dez, purple flowers. Name some."

"What?" As incredulous as Sully had ever heard him sound.

"I'm serious. Purple flowers."

"Okay, uh … Mom always grows irises."

Breanna unfolded her hands and the flower slipped from between them, fluttering to the floor. Yet, there was no further response, no unbarring of the door. All that remained was the little sparrow that, its head clearing, was beginning to struggle against Sully's gentle grip.

"The bird. It means something too, doesn't it?"

Her glassy eye remaining fixed on him. Or through him. It was impossible to tell.

Back to the name game. "It's a sparrow, right?"

And, just like that, Breanna was gone.

Hearing a click behind him, he turned. The door opened a crack, the dull light from the landing revealing itself as a strip along the floor and wall. That strip widened fast, broken by a Dez-shaped shadow as he pushed his way inside.

"The hell, Sully? You okay?"

Sully turned to face his brother. "I'm fine." His answer sounded weak even to his own ears, the energy sucked out of him. This happened a little too often in these situations. Ghosts needed energy to manifest, to get messages across. Sometimes they got it from other sources, but Sully had discovered they liked to use him like a battery. Most of the time, he had some juice left at the end of it; sometimes they drained him completely.

Dez had seen the effects often enough to know, and he moved in, getting Sully in a solid grasp.

"Bull. You're about to pass out." Dez's eyes drifted down to Sully's hands. "What the hell is that?"

"A sparrow."

"Great. Bulldog, can you take the bird outside?"

"Screw that. I'm not touching a ghost bird."

Sully ended up holding onto the sparrow while Dez held onto him, ushering him down the stairs. Nudging past Edgar so they could reach the door to the back alley, Dez pushed the steel bar with his hip to open the door for the bird's release. They watched as it flew off into the rainy night.

Dez yanked the door shut against a gust of wind, then returned his attention to Sully, dropping his brother onto a chair and shoving his head down between his knees.

Sully's protest was muffled by his lower limbs. "I'm fine."

As usual, Dez wasn't giving in easily, and his hand remained firmly in place on the back of Sully's neck. "Stop talking and take some deep breaths."

Sully obeyed for a solid minute, nudging up against Dez when the blood had returned to its usual spot in his head.

Removing his hand, Dez dropped it onto Sully's shoulder. "Better?"

"Yeah. Do the words 'iris' or 'sparrow' mean anything to either of you?"

Dez's brows lowered, confusion clear on his face. "Bulldog's ghost likes gardening?"

But Bulldog was the one looking a little pale now. "I think I know what it means. Iris Edwards. She's a young street worker, moved into town a little while ago."

"It's a big city, Bulldog," Dez said. "What makes you think this is about her?"

"She's just this tiny little munchkin, only about sixteen or seventeen years old," Bulldog said. "Well, people like to hand out street names, you know?"

Sully saw where this was going and finished for Bulldog. "And Iris goes by Sparrow."

"Bingo," Bulldog said. "So what's the deal?"

"Good question," Dez said. "First one we need to ask, I guess, is where she is. Do you know where to find her?"

"I know where to start looking. I'll ask around."

"Just don't throw Sully's name around when you're doing the asking," Dez said. "I don't want anyone finding out where it's coming from."

Bulldog glared at Dez. "Hey. This is me. I don't screw people over."

"I know. Sorry. So why do you think Breanna would be concerned about Sparrow?"

"It could be Sparrow was involved in her death somehow," Sully said. "Maybe she was there and witnessed something. Maybe she had something to do with causing it. Or it could be Breanna's worried about her."

"Bree talked about Sparrow, sometimes," Bulldog said. "Of course, my sister met a lot of the girls the last few years since she was working with that street worker project down at The Hub."

"You mean the one that tries to get the girls off the street?" Dez asked. "I didn't know she worked there."

"Clearly you don't spend a lot of time down there," Bulldog said. "Bree practically lived at The Hub the past couple years."

"And Sparrow was going there?" Sully asked.

"I know I've seen her around the place. I'll talk to a few people, see if I can get some better answers. But first thing tomorrow, okay? I'm beat."

"The couch is still yours if you want it," Sully said.

"Forget it, kid. I wouldn't go back in that room if you paid me a million bucks." Bulldog turned to Dez. "How about a ride to the Sally Ann? If they're full up, I've got a buddy on Tenth who'll give me a couch to crash on."

"Yeah, sure," Dez said. He turned to Sully. "Go get some stuff together. I'm taking you back to our place."

In all honesty, the ordered invitation sounded pretty good right now, with visions of Breanna likely to be running through Sully's head the rest of the night.

"Let me make sure everything's locked up."

He turned for the stairs and spotted Edgar, snoozing against the wall.

"Uh, Dez? Mind making one extra stop while we're at it?"

Dez appeared unconvinced. "All right, but if he pukes in my cruiser, he's riding on the hood."

4

THE SALVATION ARMY WAS FULL, as could have been expected, so Dez headed over to Tenth Street where Bulldog's friend lived.

Thankfully, Bulldog had one of those personalities that recommended him to most people, and he was welcomed in without any grumbling.

Edgar on the other hand ….

"Where to?" Dez asked, his big voice audible above the rain in a way Sully could never manage. "Hey, Eddie."

Eddie's only response was a snore from the backseat as he shifted on the hard plastic bench.

Sully reached back and slapped him on the leg. "Eddie. Hey. Last call, man."

"The usual," Edgar mumbled and emitted another car-rattling snore.

Sully met Dez's eye with an apologetic smile and an uplift of eyebrows. Dez shook his head.

"That's great, Sull. Any idea where the guy needs to go?"

"If I had my way, a detox centre, but I doubt Eddie would be too pleased about that."

"So, in other words, you don't have his address?"

"Sorry. Betty might, though."

Sully pulled out his phone and picked Betty's number out of his contacts, hitting the call button. The phone only rang once before he got her message manager. Sully gave it a couple minutes and tried again with the same outcome.

Dez provided a likely explanation. "A bunch of lines are down. Storm-related. We could head over to her place."

Sully was about to respond when a dispatcher came across Dez's radio.

"Two-six to four-seven and four-twelve."

Dez held the button down on his radio. "Four-seven."

"Nine-three-five-zero at eighteen-twenty-five Poulin Avenue. Woman reported her son called from his house five minutes ago threatening suicide by hanging. She hasn't been able to get him back on the phone, and is unable to get over there to check. Says her street's flooded."

"Ten-four," Dez said, flipping on the lights and siren and taking off, windshield wipers slapping against the front window.

It took less than two minutes to reach the address, by which time the other unit called was already on scene.

"Stay in the car," Dez told Sully as he exited. "I'll be back as soon as I can."

Sully watched Dez run to meet his colleagues, two of whom were emerging from the other cruiser with ducked heads and hunched shoulders as if that would keep them dryer.

Dez had parked at a T-intersection facing the house in question, and Sully watched until the trio of officers entered the house. Then, as if the rain and the wind weren't bad enough, the storm picked up, and the house virtually disappeared.

The downpour jackhammered against the roof, the sound of it inside the car all but deafening. Sully thought he heard something from the backseat and turned to see Edgar peering at him.

"You say something, Eddie?"

"Why am I arrested?"

Sully grinned. "You're not arrested, Eddie."

Eddie scanned his surroundings before training his incredulous glare back on Sully. "Huh?"

"It's Dez's car. My brother. You know Dez."

"You mean that huge guy with the red hair?" Eddie made a
show of lifting an arm above his head to denote Dez's height,
stopping only when the roof impeded his progress.

"Yeah, that guy. He was going to give you a lift home, but he's
just taking a call first. He'll be back right away."

"Oh." The answer seemed to relax Edgar, who appeared ready
to drop back off to sleep.

"Eddie, hey."

"Mmm?"

"What's your address?"

"I don't wear a dress, kid. Not into that shit."

"Where do you live?"

Edgar grunted and thankfully replied with a street address
that popped up on Sully's phone. At least they could drop the
man off once Dez got back. Even if Dez couldn't get Sully all the
way home right away, Edgar lived not too far from here; he'd be
an easy drop-off. Sully had spent some time now and again in
Dez's cruiser or hanging around the police station, waiting on his
brother. It wasn't the worst thing for someone who lived in his
head, Sully's thoughts usually enough to keep him busy.

Sully scanned his surroundings made visible only occasionally
through short breaks in the rain and the glow of the cruisers'
lights, a post-war area in Riverview that had crumbled with time
and neglect. Once housing young families, it was now a lower-
income neighbourhood. While most families still wanted to make
a go of it, gangs had ravaged the place with graffiti tags and fear,
while drug users and street workers littered it with hypodermic
needles and used condoms. The area was frequently on the news,
the site of numerous murders, rashes of drug-related deaths, and
community clean-up initiatives intended to turn the tides.

With the power out and nothing but the two police cars' lights to go by, it appeared as bleak as most KR residents suggested. Were it not for the rain driving most indoors, there was no telling what might be lurking in the shadows.

Still Sully had the overwhelming feeling of being watched.

He turned his head and found her there.

Standing right next to his window.

Sully jumped and gave an involuntary yelp, waking Edgar who expressed his own surprise with an utterance of, "What the hell?"

Then Breanna was gone, vanishing only long enough to pop up at what looked from here, through a sheet of driving rain, to be the entrance to an alley. Sully knew without having to ask, had been at this for far too long already. She wanted him to follow.

Staying would be easier. It was warm and dry here, relatively safe. But Sully knew how this worked, had spent his youth plagued by ghosts who refused to leave him alone until he'd figured out a way to get them what they needed. Sometimes it was a simple matter of passing a message to family. Sometimes it involved a quiet word with his foster father, Flynn Braddock, well-placed as deputy police chief.

Regardless, it meant following the clues the spirits laid out for him, knowing that if he didn't, his nights would be sleepless and his days edgy.

Sully opened the glove compartment and located a flashlight. He'd need it if he was heading out in that.

Edgar wouldn't be able to get out of the car from the back, thanks to the disabled door handles, and Dez had taken the keys with him, a fortunate force of habit. While Sully didn't think Edgar would be able to climb in front and drive off, it wasn't worth the risk of Dez having to explain to a disciplinary committee how a drunk senior had made off with his police car.

"Eddie, sit tight. I have to go check something out."

"Where ya goin'?"

"I saw someone I think I know," Sully said. "If Dez gets back before I do, tell him I headed down the alley to the right and that I saw Breanna. Can you remember that?"

"Deanna?"

"Breanna, Eddie. Breanna. Got it?"

Eddie waved a hand and nodded heavily, grumbling a reply his own mother probably wouldn't have been able to understand. Hoping for the best, Sully got out of the car and clicked on the flashlight.

It took him just a few seconds to get to where Breanna was standing, and he was soaked through by the time he reached her. He pulled up his hood and swiped at his eyes, clearing them of water; when he returned his gaze to where she'd been standing, she was gone.

He spotted her again, a dim, pale glow through the rain down the back alley, and he headed toward her, trying to keep to the edges to avoid the pooling water. He was grateful for the work boots he'd picked up at a secondhand store, his feet the only remaining dry part of him.

Breanna vanished as he approached her position, appearing again a couple of houses down. Thinking about the warm protection of the car, Sully gritted his teeth as a gust of wind threatened to blow his sodden hood from his head. Sully held onto it and continued forward, bracing himself against the pelting rain.

Breanna wasn't similarly affected, of course, her hair not whipping around or dripping as his was where it escaped his hood. He reminded himself she had things far worse, haunted as she must be by what had happened to her, by her purpose in coming for him.

At last, as they approached the end of the block, she stopped, allowing Sully to catch up before she turned and walked into the unfenced and overgrown backyard of a clearly abandoned house. There were enough of those around here, some left vacant by landlords who had tired of fixing damage caused by bad tenants, others simply given up when previous owners moved on or died with no prospect of a sale. This was quite possibly one of the latter, judging by the lean to the house, suggesting structural and foundation issues bound to cost more to fix than the property was worth. Into that, Breanna stepped, disappearing into an enclosed rear porch and waiting for him there, her form visible through the rain-streaked windows.

As unpleasant as it was standing outside in the rain, Sully was even more uncomfortable with the idea of walking in there. Houses like this might have been abandoned by their owners, but that didn't by any means translate into their being empty. Many had been illegally converted into makeshift homes by squatters, while others were taken over by junkies. Most gangs relied on houses owned or legally rented by members or associates, but that wasn't to say certain illicit dealings didn't go on in places like this one, places where no one was likely to come looking.

Despite his reservations, Sully knew if he didn't follow her, she'd never stop following him.

Heaving a breath, he walked up the rickety back steps. The door to the porch was broken, making that entry an easy one. Breanna had, by now, entered the actual house and Sully could make her out through the smashed window of the back door. His view of her was unobstructed thanks to the vandalism, a good sign Sully wasn't the first to have made this trip.

Tucking his hand into his sleeve, Sully used the wet material to turn the doorknob. It gave easily in his hand, and he opened the door only far enough to slip through into a long-disused kitchen.

Breanna was to his left now, face turned toward another door and, from its position, Sully suspected it was either a pantry or a basement. He hoped for the former but knew it had to be the latter when Breanna disappeared through the door, leaving Sully to suck back his anxiety and follow.

He was greeted by a set of wooden planks serving as stairs while Breanna waited at the bottom. Sully took the stairs carefully but found they held easily.

Revealed by the beam of the flashlight, the basement was one large, undeveloped space encased by bare cement walls. Significant cracks had formed in several places, and pools of water were spreading on the equally stark cement floor. The place had the smell of age—mould, mildew and dust—and there was something else, something not quite so prevalent, lingering in the background. It took Sully only seconds to pin it down as decay. The smell of death.

As Sully stood there, trying to figure out why Breanna had summoned him here, the smell grew until it was almost unbearable. Yet he knew it wasn't his nose picking up the scent, not really. It was beyond that somehow, a smell from the past rather than the present, lingering more in consciousness than in reality.

Sully searched Breanna's face, a dull light in the gloom. "Did you die here?"

She didn't answer in words, and he wouldn't have been able to hear her anyway. Instead, she drifted back to the rear wall, disappearing behind a space occupied by a disused water heater and furnace. Sully joined her. Nothing was there, of course, not anymore. Her body had been located and long since removed, leaving no sign of her presence save a small dark spot near the wall, which Sully suspected was blood.

He could now see the signs the police had been down here, fingerprint dust coated heavily along the rear side of the furnace and water heater, while along the wall, one latex glove lay discarded on the floor.

What else she wanted him to find, he had no clue.

It occurred to Sully he hadn't heard from Dez; he fully expected his brother would have called to give him hell for wandering off in this neighbourhood late at night. The reason for the silence became clear as Sully removed his phone to find it completely dead. Whether from battery drain or fatal water damage would remain unclear until he could get it plugged in somewhere. For now, all that mattered was finding what he needed in this basement so he could get out.

"What do you want me to see?" he asked Breanna.

Without warning, she shot toward him, that one visible death-whitened eye staring through him as her bound hands came up, fingers defying the laws of physics and nature as they wrapped, ice cold and solid, around Sully's neck.

Flashlight and phone clattering to the ground, Sully grasped at his throat, struggling to pry the fingers away. She was squeezing hard enough to cut off his oxygen, but there was nothing for him to grab, his fingers finding nothing but his own constricted flesh.

He tried to back away, mind turning to the stairs, to escape from this house, from her. But he was frozen to the spot, his flight response no longer his to control.

Although she continued to hold him in her grip, he could see no hatred in her features. If anything—and he couldn't swear there was anything to see—her face was frozen into a mask of controlled fear. It was the expression some people got when facing a mad dog, while doing all in their power to remain calm, to retain the upper hand while knowing all along it would do no good. In that state, as the frenzy took hold, the dog would never listen, and it was only a matter of moments before the inevitable attack, the lock of jaws on flesh.

Unable to speak, unable to move, Sully could do nothing as his vision began to swim, the murdered woman moving and shimmering before him in the growing haze of approaching unconsciousness. He dropped to his knees—she allowed him to, he supposed—as his sight started to fade, blackening around the edges. And still she refused to let go.

Through his panic, it occurred to Sully she might have mistaken him for the man who had killed her. He shot out a desperate thought to her that it wasn't him, that he wasn't the man. Whether she heard him or not, he didn't know. Either way, she wasn't stopping.

The image before him changed through the remaining pinhole of vision. And it was no longer a woman standing over him. It was a man.

Unable to focus, just one thing stood out: a tattoo of a partially melted, lit black candle.

Sully tried to lift his eyes to see a face, but achieved no more than a glimpse of a pale blue denim button-down shirt.

Then his vision blackened completely, and his hold on the last cords of consciousness gave, sending him down into darkness.

5

THE SUICIDAL MAN had still been in the process of contemplating the sheet he'd looped over a ceiling fan when Dez and his colleagues entered his home.

Putting aside the fact the guy had to be delusional to think the ceiling fan would support his weight, it was clear he was having a breakdown. Dez's fellow officers drew the short straw tonight and were en route to the hospital with the man to have him checked out and likely admitted to the psych ward. If things went the way Dez suspected, the man might well find himself fully committed to Lockwood Psychiatric Hospital.

But any smugness Dez felt over escaping hospital babysitting duty fell away when he returned to the car.

Edgar's sound sleep in the backseat was interrupted by Dez's hand shaking his shoulder.

"Whaaaat?" he said, batting at Dez's hand.

"Eddie, wake up. Eddie!"

"Whaddya want?"

"Where's Sully?"

"Amsterdam. How the hell should I know?"

"Damn it, Eddie, focus. Where's Sully?"

Edgar emitted a protracted groan and shifted in his seat before prying his eyes open and peering into Dez's face. "Oh, yeah. A friend, he said. Something about the alley."

"A friend? What kind of friend? Sully doesn't know anyone around ...." Dez trailed off as realization dawned. "Eddie, this friend. They have a name?"

"Of course they have a name. What the hell kind of person doesn't have a name?"

"What's the name?"

"Uhh .... Jeez ...."

"Eddie, come on."

"Uh, Deanna. Yeah, that's it. Deanna."

"Son of a bitch," Dez said. There was no question Edgar had been told to say Breanna, no other reason Sully would have left the dry comfort of the cruiser in this weather and in this neighbourhood. "Which way did he go?"

Edgar pointed noncommittally to the right, in the direction of the alley that ran to the south of Poulin Avenue.

Dez pulled out his phone and dialled Sully, listened as it rang through to a message telling him the person he was trying to reach was unavailable or out of the service area. Uttering a curse under his breath, Dez checked to ensure his flashlight was working properly before reaching for the door handle.

"Stay here, Eddie. I'm going to find Sully. I'll be back soon."

Edgar had nothing of substance to say on the matter, merely grumbling incomprehensibly and turning until he could rest his cheek against the window.

Dez shook his head and got back out into the rain, hunching against it as he felt it trickling down the back of his hair and inside the back collar of his shirt.

"Damn it, Sully," he said as he clicked on the light and jogged along the back alley.

There was no immediate sign of his brother, and it occurred to Dez that Sully had likely been led inside one of the houses. The question was which one, and none of the houses along this street was a welcome prospect. And if Sully had gone into one of several abandoned structures backing onto this alley, Dez would drop-kick his scrawny ass all the way back to the car.

He was halfway down the alley when it dawned on him where he was. He'd been here a month ago, had helped with the door-to-door enquiries that routinely followed the discovery of a homicide.

Breanna Bird had been located inside a house on Poulin Avenue and, unless he was very much mistaken, it was the night-marish abandoned house he was facing.

Dez stared at the darkened house on the darkened street, imagination running wild as a clap of thunder sounded and a streak of lightning lit the sky, illuminating the house's eye-like broken windows, the rear door gaping open like a toothless mouth threatening to swallow him.

It might have been enough to send him at a brisk walk back to the cruiser, had it not been for his missing brother and the fact Dez could just make out the dull glow of barely there light coming from a basement window. Against every ghost-fearing instinct he possessed, he edged forward and brushed at the window trying to see through. It didn't help, the layer of dust on the inside creating a near-blackout curtain.

There was no way around it now.

"Damn it, Sully."

Dez stood and drew a breath deep into his lungs, holding onto it as he stepped carefully up the back steps and into a filthy kitchen that likely hadn't hosted a hot meal in close to two decades.

The beam of his light revealed an open door to his left, a set of stairs going down. And, at the bottom, a hint of light coming from what looked to be a flashlight. It was the stillness of the light that worried Dez, had him rushing down the stairs faster than he would have without the incentive of a potentially endangered loved one. Because that, right there, was the one thing Dez feared more than ghosts.

Although he'd never personally been down here before, he'd

seen the pictures of the murder scene. And so he got a shock beyond what he naturally would have when he found Sully lying motionless behind the water heater in exactly the same position as they'd found Breanna a month ago.

Dez rushed forward and knelt at Sully's side, praying for a response as he laid a couple fingers along his brother's jawline. He found a strong pulse and was equally relieved to feel the breath coming from Sully's nose.

Dez slapped his brother's cheek, gently at first and then harder, calling his name until he saw a thread of blue-grey between the dark lashes as they slowly parted.

"Sull? Sull! Hey, man, I need you to talk to me, okay?"

"M'okay, Dez."

Dez wasn't at all confident in Sully's assessment, not just yet, anyway. But now that it was clear his brother wasn't dead or dying, Dez's mind returned to their location and the very real possibility they weren't alone. Relying on the beam of his flashlight in the small room, he tried to reassure himself as much as he could. Not that it meant anything. He wouldn't be able to see Breanna if she was kneeling right in front of him.

"Damn it," Dez muttered. Then to Sully, "Can you walk? I need to get you out of here."

Sully shifted, testing his limbs. "Give me a minute. Everything's still kind of numb."

That wasn't happening, Dez wanting the hell out of here now. Tucking the extra, smaller flashlight into his pocket and his own larger one into his utility belt, Dez pulled Sully up and over his shoulder. That done, he retrieved his flashlight and used it to guide him up the stairs he hoped would bear their weight.

"Damn it, Sull. You're an idiot, you know that? What the hell's the matter with you?"

"Can we have this discussion later?" Sully asked. "I've got a headache."

"You're going to have a bigger one by the time I'm done with you."

Dez didn't bother to put Sully down at the top of the stairs, nor anywhere on the property, just wanting to put as much distance between them and the house as quickly as possible.

Dez made it to the alley faster than was likely safe given the possibility of rotting floorboards. The rain pelted them both as he continued at a brisk pace in the direction of the cruiser.

Sully shifted in his grasp. "I think I can walk now, man."

"You think or you know?"

"I won't know for sure until you put me down."

Which was all the answer Dez needed to keep pressing on as he was. Sully could walk it off later.

Dez righted his brother only once back at the car, dumping him into the passenger seat before circling to the driver's side and dropping in behind the wheel.

"You don't feel good either, huh?" Edgar asked Sully.

Dez glared at the older man in the backseat. "Don't you even think about puking in here. I'm not in the mood." He turned to Sully. "You get an address before you ran off to play paranormal detective?"

Immediate fear passed, promptly chased by anger, but Dez bit back the lecture until he'd dropped Edgar safely back at his little Riverview home.

"Why the hell would you do something that like, huh? Goddamn it, we're at the front end of the storm of the century here, and people are looking for shelter everywhere. Do you realize what you could have run into in that house?"

Sully avoided the question with one of his own. "How'd you know where to find me?"

"Yeah, that's a good question since my only clue came from a semi-conscious, slurring drunk who mentioned an alley and someone named Deanna. Then I knew exactly where I'd find you because I remembered the house where they found her was down that block."

"About that—"

"A woman was murdered in that house, man. That's the sort of crap that goes on in those places."

"I know that, okay?"

"So why'd you go there?"

"If you'd let me get a word in, I could tell you."

"All ears, Sully."

Sully launched into an explanation of what he'd seen and what had happened to him in the basement, a tale that ended the way Sully's stories usually did—with Dez wanting to crawl out of his skin.

"They can do that?" he asked, unable to hold a poker face through this new and unexpected layer of anxiety. "Physically attack you?"

"I've never had that happen before," Sully said. "Sometimes I'll feel their injuries kind of. But I've never been in a situation like this."

"'This' being a ghost trying to kill you."

"I've thought about it, man, and I don't think she was trying to kill me."

Dez scoffed. "Yeah. Because choking someone into unconsciousness is just another way of saying 'hello,' right? Anyway, how'd she do it? She's not even solid, and you said she was trying to hit Bulldog earlier but wasn't connecting."

"I'm guessing it's because of what I can do. I'm more open to them, so they can communicate with me in ways they can't with others. But that's just a guess."

"Why attack you when you're trying to help her?"

"My best guess? She wanted to show me how she died, but I think she also needed me to really know it, to see what she saw. That tattoo. Does her common law have anything like that?"

"Easy enough to check, but from what you say, it's not her husband. He's Indigenous. The guy she showed you was white."

"So Danny's telling the truth, Dez. He didn't do it."

"Sure. All we have to do now is go to Major Crimes and tell

them Breanna's ghost choked you out and showed you a tattooed arm. They'd laugh us out of there in two minutes flat."

"I guess that means I need to find something else then."

Dez glared at him. "Nope. You're done with this. It's getting too dangerous."

"I don't have a choice. I haven't met many as determined as she is. She won't stop, not with me or Bulldog, until I've finished this for her."

"And what if you can't? Sully, you're only twenty years old, you've got no background in investigation or defensive tactics, and you're talking about going up against a killer whose name and face you don't even know. He could be anyone."

"Anyone except Danny. Come on, Dez. I need to help Breanna, for my own sanity as much as anything. And you know we can't leave Danny rotting in jail for something he didn't do."

"He still hit her. Far as I'm concerned, jail's a good place for him."

"Maybe so, but there's a murderer out there getting away with it right now. For all we know, he could be getting ready to kill again."

"And how certain are you that you won't end up being his next victim?"

"Dez, you can't protect me forever."

Dez met his eye. "No? Watch me."

There was nothing Sully could say to that, no arguing with Dez on a characteristic as much a part of him as his hair colour or height. They fell back into silence as Dez drove Sully to his home in the Gladstone neighbourhood and pulled into the driveway.

Dez snagged his brother's arm as he tried to climb out of the car. "I know I can get overbearing with you, and I'm sorry. But it won't change. That said, I know we need to do this—and I mean 'we.' You stay put at my place tonight and then tomorrow morning we'll start figuring some stuff out."

Sully met his eye with a smile. "Thanks, bro."

Dez smiled in reply, but it faded fast. "And if you even think of leaving this house without me at your back on this, ghosts and murderers will be the least of your problems. You got me?"

WHEN SULLY AWOKE in Dez and Eva's spare bedroom, sunlight was streaming through the windows, and Breanna was standing over him.

It took the usual few seconds for his heart to stop pounding as he fixed her with a glare. "I'm on it, okay? By the way, that choking thing last night kind of sucked."

Eva had gotten up briefly to say hi last night and had commented on the bruises around his throat, at which point Sully realized Breanna's attack had been a little more physical than he'd realized.

This morning was no better. The bruises had deepened in places, two dark spots the shape of thumb pads directly in the centre of his throat.

A little before eight, Sully found Eva in the kitchen, struggling to settle their energetic three-year-old long enough to get a full breakfast in her. Kayleigh was a cute kid by any standard, but she also possessed an exotic appearance by virtue of her mother's Indigenous hair and skin colouring and her father's Irish green eyes. In attitude, as Eva frequently observed, Kayleigh was every inch her father's daughter: stubborn and strong and yet affectionate and open, with a healthy dose of wacky humour tossed in. Eva was far steadier with her emotions than either her husband or daughter, a rock for Dez's waves to crash against. Dez was prone to an emotional gamut of giddying highs and depressive lows, but Sully had noticed his brother had been far more even-keeled since he'd met Eva. And for someone who loved his brother as much as Sully did, that made Eva a godsend.

It didn't hurt that Dez had his own family to fuss over now, giving Sully the advantage of a little more breathing space. Without Eva, the very notion of Sully's working late hours at a bar in Riverview would have led to countless arguments with Dez and far more and longer visits during his shifts. While Dez was still plenty protective of him—a reality Sully quietly didn't mind given his once-lonely and neglected past—Sully could recognize and appreciate the recently afforded room to spread his wings a little. For a guy straddling that border between youth and manhood, that was a welcome change.

Sully grinned as Kayleigh's eyes lit up at the sight of her uncle. Eva gave up the battle as Kayleigh sprung from the chair and bounded over, arms extended as she angled for a hug. Sully happily obliged, scooping her up and holding her to him.

"Hey, KayBee, how's my girl?"

"Hi, Unca Suh-wee!" she exclaimed, tiny arms clamping around his neck like a vice. Her father's daughter indeed.

Sully peered over Kayleigh's head at Eva. "Dez get home okay?"

"Soaked through and grumpy, but he was a happy camper by the time he showered and hit the mattress. You sleep all right?"

"Like a log. I thought you worked today."

"I'm going to a swing shift for a few days," she said. "Dez is moving to nights."

That would work well for having Dez's help on the Breanna thing, for the moment at least. After that, it would be a matter of either falling back on Mara Braddock to watch Kayleigh, or Sully trying to find a way to get out of the house without Dez threatening to tie him to something. Sully had a feeling there would be no place for Kayleigh in an impromptu murder investigation.

"How's the throat?" Eva asked, moving closer for a look.

"It doesn't really hurt that bad. It looks worse than it is."

"Sounded pretty bad from what Dez told me."

"He was pretty freaked out about it."

Eva's smile was a knowing one. "You don't say. Do you mind working your magic to get Kayleigh to eat? She actually listens to you and, that way, I can start on the big people's breakfast."

Sully sat down with Kayleigh on his knee, spooning the crispy rice cereal into her mouth while she eyed him and giggled between bites.

"Still raining?" he asked, glancing out the window next to where Eva was readying a couple frying pans on the stove.

"Pouring. We're lucky we've still got power out here. A lot of places more city centre are still out. The wind's not as bad, so they said on the news this morning crews are trying to patch up the broken lines. That said, it's likely the wind's going to pick up again later today. So will the rain, if you can believe that."

"Are they still talking about evacuating The Forks?"

"Possibly. The Forks is still on high alert, and some people have already left just in case. The river's higher, already, and the beach is underwater again, but so far no major flooding to the houses. Lots of sump pumps and sandbags working overtime, though."

Sully made an airplane noise for Kayleigh, flying another spoonful of cereal into the open hangar. As Kayleigh chewed, Sully returned his attention to Eva, and to the topic of Breanna.

"Eva, did you know a woman named Breanna Bird?"

"Yeah. It was awful what happened to her. She was a pretty awesome woman." She turned to meet Sully's eye. "You're sure it was Breanna who attacked you last night? It doesn't seem like something she'd do."

Sully pictured his close-up view of the woman's face, the blackened, cloudy eye staring through him as she implanted that image in his brain immediately before unconsciousness. "I'm sure. Like I told Dez, she wasn't trying to hurt me, just show me something."

"Granted, I was half-asleep, and we didn't have a long conversation about it, but he mentioned something to me about her showing you a guy with a tattoo on his forearm?"

"A black candle, yeah. Lit and dripping wax. Have you ever come across something like that?"

"If I did, I don't remember it. I can run a check when I get to work, see if we've got anyone in the database with that tattoo."

"That would be awesome, thanks."

Eva cracked a few eggs into one of the pans. "Scrambled or fried?"

"Doesn't matter to me."

Eva set about scrambling. She was silent a few minutes as Sully listened to Kayleigh's chatter, but she spoke up while her daughter was busy chewing.

"You need to be more careful, Sully. No repeats of what happened last night, okay?"

Sully was trying to think up a decent explanation that wouldn't negate an apology when Eva turned to face him. "Dez will follow you anywhere. You know that. I get the things you see and feel must be pretty intense, and that you want them over as soon as possible. I really do. But, if you jump without thinking it through first, you're not only putting yourself at risk, but Dez too. I know he can hover, and it can get frustrating. Believe me, he does the same with us. But it's who he is."

"I know it is. You're right. I'm sorry. I wasn't thinking last night."

"It's not just about Dez. It's you too. Dez loves you but so do Kayleigh and I and your parents. Just try to remember that before you leap, all right?"

Sully nodded and smiled. There wasn't a whole lot else he could do.

He could promise her all sorts of things, but he knew there were times when cautious delay wasn't an option. Not with the people he was dealing with.

Sometimes they made the decisions for him.

6

DEZ DIDN'T SLEEP MUCH LONGER, the smell of frying bacon proving enough to draw him out of bed.

Sully was on the floor with Kayleigh, playing with a firetruck one of Dez and Eva's friends had given her for her last birthday. A rescue only Kayleigh could see paused briefly as Dez scooped her up and kissed her on the forehead.

"Sweetie, I thought we agreed you wanted to be a police officer, not a firefighter."

Kayleigh beamed. "Fire, Daddy!"

Dez made a face and set her back down. "Whose kid are you, anyway?"

Kayleigh laughed that off, then broke into a fresh set of giggles as Dez walked past and ruffled Sully's hair before moving to the stove to kiss Eva good morning.

"Smells good, babe."

"You want to help me out, grab a spatula, Snowman. Bacon duty's on you."

Eva had been calling Dez "Snowman" since they'd met, presumably a reference to the abominable snowman rumoured to be only slightly bigger than Dez himself. Sully had tried repeating the nickname at Dez once and had been soundly throttled for it.

There were some things only a beautiful woman could get away with.

After breakfast was done and the dishwasher loaded, Dez dropped back into his chair at the table while Eva carried Kayleigh off for a bath.

Sully, still at the table, waited until he and Dez were alone. "What's up?"

"I had a chance last night to check our system for that tattoo you mentioned. Only one guy shows as having something like that. His name's Kenton Barwell, and he's bad news. He's a known gun and drug dealer with a history of violence, and he's known to carry a concealed firearm. He's not believed to be a patched-in member of any particular gang, but he's a known associate of the Devil's Cross."

"How close an associate exactly?"

"Too close for comfort," Dez said. "He was netted during a couple of gang-house raids over the past few years, so he's definitely close enough to get in the door and leave again intact."

"So what's the best plan for talking to him?"

"Huh?"

"We're going to have to talk to him. That's the only way to find out whether he's the right guy."

Sully knew he was right on that last point when Dez limited his argument to the former. "You, little brother, are not going anywhere near Kenton Barwell, you got me? I'll check him out."

"You just said he's been known to carry. You may be able to take him easily in a fair fight, but you make a pretty sizeable target if he decides to shoot first. Anyway, I'm the one who saw the tattoo, so unless you're able to convince him to let you photograph his arm, you've got no choice but to take me with you."

Dez sat back in the chair, crossing him arms over his chest while fixing Sully with a firm glare—Dez's patented immovable object pose.

"Not happening, Sully. End of story."

"So what do we do about it then? I need to figure this out, and

I can't think of any other way. If that tattoo is the key to all of this, I need to see it."

Dez had yet to uncross his arms or to release Sully from that piercing stare. And Sully was well aware Dez was thinking back on his brother's ill-advised adventure last night and wondering to what lengths he might need to go to prevent any sort of repeat.

"Dez …."

"There might be another way," Dez said, sitting forward and propping his arms on the table—a position that held more promise for Sully. "Paul Dunsmore. You know him?"

"He opened one of the shelters in Riverview, Rising Son."

"Yeah, but it's a little more than that. He used money from his day job with his family's business to start a program called End of the Tunnel. It's kind of turned it into a catchall over the years, handles mobile crisis, some street life extraction, stable housing, education, employment. Paul's basically become a brother to some of the older street people and a surrogate father to the younger ones. He's plugged in in a way few are. Be worth an ask, I think."

"He'd know about people's tattoos?"

"Not necessarily, but he'd be able to ask in a way that wouldn't end with him nursing a bullet wound. Anyway, he'd be a good guy for you to know. Chances are he knows exactly where guys like Edgar live and would be happy to pop by the bar next time and play cabbie."

Dez checked his watch. "As you can imagine, Paul keeps some goofy hours, so I doubt he'd be down at the shelter or at Tunnel offices yet. And I think I remember someone telling me his day job involves mainly working from home." He met Sully's eye and smiled. "I'm sure he'd be thrilled if we turned up on his doorstep, though."

———

SULLY, like everyone else in Riverview, knew of Paul.

But, while the man had popped in at the Black Fox on a few occasions, Sully had never had occasion to get to know the man.

So he was surprised when Dez steered them out of Riverview and north on the Forks Bridge. Were it not for the persistent heavy rain, they'd have a spectacular view right now of the beach and, to the east, the expanse of land that made up what was called The Forks. The area was home to some of the oldest and most beautiful residences in the city, as well as the priciest boutique shopping and the most exclusive restaurants. It was where the old rich lived, played, retired and eventually died, an area as exclusive as a country club where only the right kind were granted a welcome.

"Seems like a weird place to find Paul Dunsmore," Sully said.

"Is, isn't it? There are a few things about him that might surprise you."

"Such as?"

"His father, for starters. You know Dunsmore Developments?"

Sully shook his head.

"You really need to pay more attention to the news. That's the corporation that broke land on a large chunk of the buildings going up in New Town." Dez tweaked a thumb backwards, toward the growing number of glass towers that were transforming KR's relatively new downtown core, a replacement for the Riverview area that had—as far as the "respectable" were concerned—given way to the wrong sort. "Dunsmore Developments designed the buildings and then the corporation held the contracts on the physical construction. They've had their hands in New Town development right from the start and, judging by the height of their tower, they're doing pretty well for themselves."

"So Paul's father runs Dunsmore?"

"Mother and father. It's a family affair. The whole lot of them, including Paul, have a seat on the board, and Paul works in architecture or design or something. But I'm told he avoids the office whenever possible."

"His choice or theirs?"

"Word is he's kind of a black sheep but, honestly, I'm not sure of much beyond that. Could be he wants to put as much distance as possible between himself and the business while still raking in the cash. I remember a few issues cropping up between the Dunsmores and social activists or history lovers when plans were tabled to tear down historic buildings and affordable housing to make way for New Town development. You can see who won that battle. That's what pushed so many more folks east into Riverview, which was just fine with the likes of the Dunsmores."

"But not Paul."

"He's used his money to set up various foundations and social programs. The Rising Son shelter was just one of them. As far as Riverview goes, he's got the golden touch. Everyone wants to be near him—which is why he might be the right guy to get us the info we need. There aren't a lot of people on either side of the financial spectrum who will say no to Paul Dunsmore."

Sully regarded his wardrobe of baggy hooded sweatshirt, jeans and scuffed work boots, then flipped down the visor to check his hopeless mop of pale brown hair. He hadn't shaved this morning, leaving him with a layer of stubble that girls liked more than wealthy businessmen were likely to.

Dez smirked at him. "Don't worry, Sull. One look at that pretty face and Dunsmore will be the bluebird sitting on your shoulder. I hear he's got a thing for cute young guys. Especially scruffy ones like you."

Sully didn't often pay much attention to people's clothing choices. It had taken him until this moment to really notice what his brother had put on: crisp, gray slacks and a subtly shiny, pale gray button-down under his black waterproof jacket.

Dez read Sully's thoughts as well as his sightline. "Hey, at least one of us needed to look respectable."

Sully backhanded Dez, giving him a solid whack on the shoulder. Dez rubbed at the spot and laughed. "Not like I've got anything to fit your tiny ass, bro. I can't help it you dress like a hoodlum."

Dez stopped laughing long enough to cast Sully a sidewise

glance, dropping his tone back to serious. "Look, I get you have a thing about rich people. But you'll be fine, all right? Believe me, Paul Dunsmore is the last guy in this city who will give a damn."

On the other side the bridge, Dez took the off-ramp onto Oldwater Road, the route that ran a perimeter around most of the island. They hadn't gone far when Dez was forced to detour further north, a portion of the pavement having been washed out.

"Jesus, I can only imagine what the next city council meeting's going to sound like," Dez said. "Something in The Forks always washes out in a storm. I swear, nothing will ever get done anywhere in KR again what with the island and New Town sopping up all the tax dollars."

They headed east for a while until Dez deemed it safe to drop back onto Oldwater.

"I'm guessing he has a waterfront place?" Sully asked.

"Nothing but the best for a Dunsmore," Dez said with a smirk. "Do me a favour. Check the GPS on my phone. I programmed in the address after I looked it up on the DMV."

Sully checked his brother's phone and watched as the blue dot indicating their location neared the destination point. At Sully's direction, Dez pulled in next to a large metal gate and put his window down so he could press the call button. They were rewarded with a blast of rain and a voice coming over the speaker.

"Yes?"

"Paul Dunsmore?"

"Yes."

"Desmond Braddock and Sullivan Gray."

Sully expected further explanation would be required and was surprised to see the gates parting and opening inward, allowing them entry. Dez finished putting up his window and shrugged at Sully's questioning gaze.

"Beats me," Dez said. "I barely know the guy."

A short drive led to the house, a large two-storey brick colonial surrounded by a manicured yard and bordered by stands of elm, poplar and evergreen trees. Paul stood in the open doorway, and he waved Dez and Sully over with a rapid gesture as they got out of the vehicle. Despite their quicker pace, both were wet by the time they reached the door.

Paul was every inch the off-duty business tycoon in a crisp pair of chinos and a long-sleeved sweater that looked like it was made of material too expensive to snag. His blond hair managed to appear both tousled and perfectly set, and his welcoming grin revealed teeth so white they could probably be seen in the dark.

"It's a real mess out there," Paul said, ushering the brothers inside. "Come in and make yourselves comfortable. I'll put on some coffee."

Sully met Dez's eye, certain his suspicion showed. Sully was a lot of things, but trusting wasn't one of them and Dez, coming to the rescue with a reassuring smile, knew it.

"I'm not sure we've had a chance to properly meet you," Dez said to Paul's retreating back.

Paul paused long enough to turn with a friendly grin. "Well, clearly you know who I am, and I know who you are, so that's that settled." Dez was the one appearing confused now, drawing a chuckle from their host. "For starters, I've met Sullivan at the Black Fox. And, more obviously, my family does business with your uncle Lowell."

Sully blanched at the name. Lowell was the only Braddock he could live without. Flynn's brother had his own pharmaceutical and research company, and LOBRA now had its head office in one of the swankiest buildings in New Town, while its lab and research wing was housed in a similarly pricy compound on the city's east side. Lowell was rolling in the dough and, while he came off as warm and personable, Sully knew better.

"What business is that?" he asked.

Paul's answering smile was a little more than friendly. Sully had recognized him upon entering the house as a man he had encountered at the Fox a handful of times, and he was fairly convinced the drunken butt grab from a few weeks ago was not quite as accidental as Paul had made out.

"LOBRA's head office is in one of my family's buildings," Paul said. "And my family designed and constructed the research facility for Lowell. He seems like a good guy."

Sully caught on the words "seems like," reading between the lines in a way Dez likely wouldn't. Dez was a smart guy, a people guy, and he was typically good at reading others. But Lowell was a blind-spot for him—for all the Braddocks—and so Sully found his respect for Paul heightening a notch or two.

This time, Sully wasn't so reluctant at Paul's insistence they join him in the kitchen for coffee. Tastefully decorated, the kitchen had been outfitted with butcher-block countertops and classic white cupboards; a heavy sliding glass door led out to a covered patio, which the driving rain currently rendered unusable. Beyond that, barely visible due to the storm, the wide expanse of the South Kimotan looked deceptively calm while its banks gradually swelled and its below-the-surface currents raged.

Dez, something of an aficionado for construction, wandered over to pound lightly on the wall keeping them separated from the pounding storm. "This is amazing. You can barely hear the wind out there."

"Noise-cancelling," Paul said as he busied himself with the coffeemaker. "My father's a light sleeper. When he built this place, he made sure to use the best materials available. There's better on the market now, mind you, but this does well enough for my purposes. When I have a party, you can barely make out noise between floors, and it's not even bad room to room. My dad's idea. Besides being a light sleeper, my brother snores like you wouldn't believe."

Dez left the wall alone and joined Sully at the kitchen's sizeable island, sliding onto one of three barstools that lined the side facing the patio.

"I thought your parents had a place further up the island," Dez said.

"Oh, they do. This is their old place. They wanted something new that was better befitting their lifestyle. They decided this place was too small for them."

Sully guessed his face said everything Dez's was because Paul chuckled as he glanced between them. "Don't worry. I share your views. This house is plenty big for any normal, rational human being. Money does all sorts of things to people's brains. The weird thing is, it costs money to be rich if it's important to you that everyone sees you as such. As for me, there are better things to do with my money—not least of all fixing some of the mess my family's projects helped create."

"You still do some work for the family business, don't you?" Dez asked.

"Architectural design. And, yes, I'm well-paid for my efforts, despite the fact I have difficulty keeping my trap shut around there."

"You're probably wondering why we're here."

"I'd rather hoped it was for my sparkling conversation and other personal charms."

Dez's answering laugh suggested a measure of comfort while Sully worked on a grin that would pass muster. He wasn't big on sparkling conversation at the best of times. Dez was the people guy, possessing a deep, booming voice and a laugh to match; Sully often had to be asked to repeat himself. The best thing about the Black Fox—besides the fact it meant a home and a job for a guy recently out of high school with no real skills besides playing the guitar and communicating with the dead—was the fact few people came there to chat. And those who did were genuine. What you saw, you got, and what you got was a lack of pretence and put-ons, people who just wanted a drink and a think. The sports bars and nightclubs were for socializing. The Fox was where you went when you wanted the world to leave you the hell alone.

The job was the only truly good thing Lowell had ever done for him.

"We're actually looking for some information, and we thought you might be able to help us out," Dez said.

Paul left the coffeemaker to its business and joined the brothers at the island, leaning forward against it—the picture of curiosity and openness. "What is it you need?"

"Your discretion, for starters," Dez said. "I'm a police officer, but I'm not acting in an official capacity here, just making inquiries for a friend. I'm hoping I can count on you to keep this visit between us."

Paul leaned further forward, settling his upper body onto folded arms. "I'm intrigued."

"Did you know Breanna Bird?"

Sully saw a subtle change in Paul's face, the shifting of a few muscles that caused the edges of his smile to droop.

"Yes, I knew her," he said. "She was wonderful. She did such fantastic work with the Street Worker Exit Strategy that I actually ended up providing a significant donation. I was heartbroken when she died. All those years she spent on the street, all the drugs, all those close shaves with bad johns, and it's her husband who ends up killing her."

"That's actually the problem right there," Dez said. "We came across some intel that another man might have been involved, one with a distinctive tattoo. Actually, it only comes up on the police system once. We're following up on the lead, and we're hoping you might recognize it or could keep your eyes open."

"What sort of tattoo?"

"It's a lit black candle on his forearm," Sully said. "Some dripping wax around it. Sound like anything you've seen?"

Paul pinched at his lower lip, his face showing him deep in thought. Finally, he returned his gaze to Sully. "I'm sorry, I can't think of anyone I know with something like that. And I've seen my share of tattoos with the people I know from Rising Son or The Hub. There wasn't anything else? It seems strange you'd have just a tattoo to go by. Wouldn't your source have seen a little more than that?"

"That's all we've got, other than that we're looking for a white guy," Dez said.

"Who's your source, if you don't mind me asking?"

"Sorry," Dez said. "We can't say. I'm sure you understand."

"Of course. I shouldn't have asked."

"No offence," Dez said. "Listen, I had one name come up on the system, a Kenton Barwell. You ever hear of him?"

"It sounds vaguely familiar."

"Could be some folks around there have talked about him. He's known to trade in drugs and black market firearms."

"I can't say that most of the people I see day to day have anything much to do with him. I'm probably safe to assume he's not a street-level dealer?"

"No, I'd say he's nearer the middle of the heap, maybe even closer to the top at this point. He's wholesale, not a street dealer."

"Then he'd be a little out of my usual range. But I can ask around."

"Don't," Dez said. "Last thing I want is for Barwell to find out you're throwing his name around. He's not likely to take it well and I'd rather you don't get caught in any crossfire on this. We'd appreciate it if you could just see if you can find out if anyone else has a tattoo like the one Sully described. I'll leave you my number in case you catch wind of anything."

Dez didn't seem to be in any rush to get back outside, taking his time with the coffee Paul provided a few minutes later. The wind, already reasonably strong this morning, had picked up, and Sully suspected any existing repairs to power and phone lines would be rendered short-lived.

"The river's getting pretty high out there," Dez said to Paul. "You sure you're still safe to stay here? A few Forks residents are making for higher ground as we speak."

Paul, seated on a barstool adjacent to Sully, followed their gaze to the river before waving a dismissive hand at it. "Ach, it'll be fine. People around here get panicky at the first sign of heavy rain.

This is home. I've got everything here. It would be a huge pain in the ass to have to leave."

"Still," Dez said. "It's probably a good idea to have an exit strategy."

Paul grinned. "As my father always says, exit strategies are for the weak. It's sticking it out that makes the man."

7

HEADED BACK into the city centre, Dez let Sully take the wheel so he could start making some calls.

The first one had them changing course, a return to Gladstone delayed in favour of a trip downtown.

"There's no way we can get in to see Breanna's common-law husband without setting off about a hundred alarm bells," Dez told Sully. "But Danny's lawyer's willing to talk to us."

The Legal Aid office was located in a brick office tower on the side of New Town that had so far been left more or less untouched. It was there, in the area that bordered Riverview, that some of the city's most necessary civic structures—city hall, the court building, police headquarters, main fire hall, General Hospital, central library and the train and bus station—were located, making it hard to demolish the older buildings to make way for the new. Thankfully, most structures in that area had the classic facades that made them worth keeping, even to those who preferred the shiny and new.

Dez had spent enough time in the Justice building during the few years he'd been with the KRPD, mainly visiting the prosecutors' offices that took up a couple floors near the top—just below the uppermost floors that housed the Justice Ministry and its various officials.

Legal Aid was on the first two floors, and it was on the second that they found Olivia Tan, known for her slight build and large courtroom presence.

It was possible that if she gained a few pounds, she might be half Dez's size, but she still met his handshake with a solid grip that made his own conscious attempt at a light touch seem overly soft and unnecessary.

"Thanks for meeting with us," he said. "Not sure if you remember me from court, but I'm—"

"Desmond Braddock," she finished. "And I'm sorry. I kind of tore into you on the witness stand the last time we met."

"You remember that, huh?"

"Just doing my job for my client. But, for the record, you seem like a decent guy and a good cop." Her eyes turned to Sully, and Dez made the introductions.

Olivia studied the two of them in turn, eyebrows raised. Dez had grown used to that a long time ago. "You two are brothers?"

"Foster brothers, technically," Sully said. "The Braddocks took me in when I was seven."

Dez allowed Sully's explanation before adding his own. "And he's been blood ever since. Listen, thanks for meeting us on such short notice."

"You told me over the phone you were working on something that could benefit Danny Newton. You're aware, I'm sure, that he's tried to retract his statement to investigators."

"We'd heard. Any chance we might be able to have a look at it?"

"Since you're not acting officially, and I haven't had a chance to clear the particulars with my client, I'm not at liberty to share it with you, unfortunately. But I don't see why I can't speak with you, unofficially—provided, of course, this stays between us for the time being. I can't discuss my conversations with Danny, but I can provide you with some background. This has pretty much all been said in open court anyway."

Dez and Sully dropped into the well-used, lightly padded chairs Olivia waved them to, Dez trying to avoid leaning back against the seat where his wet jacket would leave its mark. Not that it would matter all that much. Plenty of other butts and backs had been in these chairs, and it showed.

Olivia lowered herself into a comfortable-looking leather swivel that was wearing at the seams despite the tiny weight it had to bear. "Before I get into what I've got, would you mind telling me about this potential evidence?"

Dez provided the explanation, wanting to leave Sully out of it as much as possible. Olivia had a brain that ran about a hundred miles a minute and she was known to sense a liar even before one took the oath on the witness stand. Dez was used to the courtroom and, while he was a lousy liar, he had developed the skill of providing only what information was necessary. Now he stuck to the line about source information and avoided the questionable parts—specifically details about how they'd come by information about the tattoo.

"Source information, you say," she said once he'd finished. "How reliable is the source?"

"Reliable," Dez said. There was no question. He'd seen Sully in action over the years, had heard him come up with descriptions that defied logic. He'd once described a stabbing victim right down to the colour and style of his clothes and the number and location of wounds—and that was before anyone had located the body. Thankfully, that guy had left Sully alone once police found his remains and arrested his killer.

"And are the police looking into it?"

"In a way," Dez said. "I'm looking into it."

"No offence, Constable, but you're in patrol. I would think this would require some work by someone in Major Crimes."

"The information's a little sensitive at this point," Dez said. "The source is reluctant to come forward."

Olivia's hawklike eyes next turned to Sully. "I'm guessing you're the source."

Damn. "Sully knows the source," Dez said before his brother could answer. As of now, Dez could count on one hand the number of people who knew what Sully could do, and he was keen to keep it that way for his brother's sake. God only knew the kind of fruitcakes that would creep out of the woodwork if Sully was publicly outed. Then there was the fact investigators were unlikely to look favourably on the intrusion of a psychic in the midst of a case they'd put to bed. With the likes of Sgt. Forbes Raynor in the lead investigator role, Sully would be raked over the coals before anyone deemed his information worthy—if they ever deemed it worthy.

For his part, Dez planned on ensuring they had some concrete evidence to present to investigators before they took it forward.

Olivia smiled and nodded knowingly, despite Dez's best attempts at fibbing. But Dez held his tongue, and Sully was doing likewise next to him—an easier feat for Sully at the best of times.

Whether she'd been expecting further information or had decided it was all the answer she needed was anyone's guess. Whatever the case, Olivia didn't press further on that count.

"The two of you will go forward with your findings once you get something concrete?" she asked.

"We will," Dez said.

"All right. That's good enough for me, I suppose. I've approached the Crown's office, asking them to have Major Crimes look into my client's claims; so far, I'm unconvinced anything of note has happened. No one has gone to reinterview Danny yet, which I find disturbing. I think the powers that be think Danny's just back-pedalling now that he sees a life sentence looming, and they don't want to waste resources given other investigations."

"What is it they have on Danny exactly?"

"Not much. According to the disclosure I've received, all they really have is his confession and her blood at their house.

Granted, that's a lot typically, but it also fits with his new explanation."

"Which is?"

Olivia leaned forward, knitting her fingers atop her desk as she launched into the story. "Danny and Breanna met about a decade ago when they were both in their early-to-mid-twenties. They lived hard back then, but they decided to work together to get themselves cleaned up. And they worked their asses off at it. There were a few slips. A look at either of their criminal records will tell you that. But overall, they held the course, and both have been sober for close to five years now. As you may be aware, Breanna has been heavily involved in helping people on the street, particularly young street workers trying to change their lives. Danny got his high-school equivalency and started working in the construction trade. He'd been very busy and had been pulling in some decent money for them.

"But then Danny fell off the wagon. He swears to me, as he told police, it was just the one time. It was a co-worker's birthday and they all went out for the night. You can guess how things went. Danny bowed to peer pressure. He told me he thought he'd be okay if he just nursed one for the night. But one of the guys started buying rounds, and then shots. And the next thing he knew, he was under the table.

"Danny remembers heading home and the inevitable fight with Breanna. She was a kind woman, but tough, he said, and that was one of the biggest reasons he stayed on the wagon all that time. But all you have to do is look at Danny's record to see he's a different person when he's drinking. He's soft-spoken and thoughtful sober, but drunk, he's got a history of assault against anyone within reach—domestic partners, friends, strangers, police, it didn't matter. I'm afraid that's why the police and the Crown don't believe him now.

"Anyway, everything gets a little fuzzy for Danny around the time he left the bar. He isn't sure how he got home, and he doesn't remember when he got there. He's got a recollection of the argument, but not all of it. The last thing he remembers is punching Breanna in the face. He thinks she must have fallen and hit her head, because there was a bloodstain there the next morning. But no Breanna. She was just gone."

"I don't remember there being a missing person report," Dez said.

Olivia shook her head. "He didn't file one. He just thought she left him. He says he called a few of her family members but everyone told him they hadn't seen her. He thought it was very possible they were lying to him to protect Breanna, so he went to see a few of them. The investigation confirmed all that. It also confirmed he went to The Hub to see if she had been there, and he was told no. He says he considered filing a missing person report at that point, but ultimately didn't. She knew a lot of people he didn't through her work, and he believed she had gone to stay with a friend he didn't know. He figured she'd turn up again soon."

"But she was injured," Dez said. "He wasn't worried about that?"

"There wasn't so much blood that it would be worrying. He thought she was well enough to get up and leave, so she had to have been okay. A couple days later, someone found her body in the basement of an abandoned house. Obviously, investigators looked at Danny first. By then, he had fallen completely off the wagon and he put up a fight with police in what I believe was an attempt at suicide-by-cop. But police took him in safely and he's been in custody since.

"To say Danny was shattered would be putting it mildly. Breanna was his whole world, his reason for living. He's got a teenaged daughter somewhere, but he lost custody and never sought it again after he sobered up. He told me there are no words to describe the level of guilt he felt that he started drinking again, that he let Breanna down so badly, that he hurt her physically and emotionally, that he didn't report her missing. And he has no memory. For a while, he actually believed what the police were telling him in the interview room, that he might well have killed her. And so he provided a confession."

"What exactly was this confession?" Dez asked.

"Exactly nothing, to be frank. He said he thinks he must have killed her. End of story. Sgt. Raynor showed Danny photos of Breanna's body at the scene, and by the time the questioning was over, Danny had admitted to tying her up and strangling her. It means nothing. Anyone looking at those photos could see she was bound and had bruises around her neck. He didn't tell them anything they didn't provide to him in some way. And Danny couldn't give them an address and police were never able to connect him to that location in any way."

"Who owns the house?"

"A slumlord, essentially. The place was left in a bad state by the last tenants and he decided it wasn't worth fixing up again. He's got numerous other properties, including an apartment building, that are earning him money. He's not worried about that house, so it's just been abandoned. Now it's used for all sorts of negative purposes—drugs, prostitution, gang activity and, obviously, murder."

"So Raynor's theory is what? That Danny punched Breanna and then blacked out, took her to this other house and killed her?"

"Not exactly. Police don't believe Danny blacked out. They think he's making that bit up to angle for a manslaughter conviction by alleging he had the inability to form the intent for murder. The Crown's theory is that she took off after he hit her, and he chased or followed her, then killed her in the house where she was found. It's a couple of blocks from their home. Only no one reported hearing any commotion or seeing anyone running down the street."

"That might not mean anything around there," Dez said. "I responded to a shooting in that neighbourhood a couple months ago, and no one heard the gunshot. When bad stuff becomes common, people stop noticing."

Olivia smiled sadly. "Unfortunately, what you say makes complete sense."

"How long was it between the fight with Danny and her body being found?" Sully asked.

"Two days. And there was some decomposition beginning already, so it's believed she died the night of the fight with Danny. The pathologist can't give an exact time of death, so it's possible she died sometime the following day."

"I know Sully and I have our doubts," Dez said. "But I'm curious, what makes you so sure Danny didn't do it?"

"Between you and me, Constable, I'm not," Olivia said. "But he's sure, and he's my client. He said he loves her more than his own life, that there's no way he could have killed her. Not in any state. And if there's anything I'm sure of, it's that he genuinely feels that way. My job is not necessarily to see him acquitted, it's to ensure the Crown's case is solid and that all the avenues have been explored. I don't think I need to tell you I've got umpteen other cases on my plate at the moment. I don't have the time or resources I wish I had to devote to Danny, so all the help you can provide is more than welcome. It may be a long shot, but if this tattoo thing goes anywhere, please let me know."

Olivia scanned her watch face, and Dez took that as their cue to exit.

"Thanks for your time," he said, standing.

"No, thank you," she said, reaching out to shake his hand.

Sully stood slowly, taking the hand Olivia offered, but not letting go right away. "Can I ask you one more question? Danny's daughter. By any chance is her name Iris Edwards?"

"Yes, it is. How did you know that?"

Sully released the lawyer's hand, his expression suggesting a smile that didn't quite get there.

"A little bird, I guess," he said.

8

"How'd you know to ask about Sparrow?" Dez asked once he and Sully were back in the SUV, rain pounding off the roof and the windshield, obscuring the grey city outside the vehicle.

Sully massaged at his temples, trying to ease away a mounting headache. "It just occurred to me. Breanna's so determined we find Sparrow, I just figured there might be something more to it."

"Bulldog never mentioned Sparrow was his niece," Dez said.

"Maybe he doesn't know. She isn't Breanna's daughter, after all. Sparrow would have been born a few years before Danny and Breanna even met."

"But it seems like Breanna cared about her, right? I mean, she must if she's going all in to have us find her." Dez checked his watch. "Damn. Eva's going to be leaving for work pretty quick. I need to get home to watch Kayleigh."

"We're not far from The Hub," Sully said. "I'll head over there and ask around about Sparrow, see if anyone knows anything about her."

"No, Sull. No way."

"Dez—"

"You're not doing this by yourself."

"I'm never exactly by myself, you know."

Sully glanced over in time to catch Dez's glare. "Yeah, well, I'm not counting a ghost who strangled you as adequate backup, all right?"

"Dez, if everything turns out the way I think it's heading, then this Sparrow girl's in big trouble. You know there's no time to waste on this."

"No offence to Sparrow, but it's you landing in big trouble I'm more worried about." But Dez's sigh suggested some resignation. "Look, I'll drop you off at the Hub as long as Bulldog meets us there, okay? I'll head home and take Kayleigh to Mom's, and then I'll come and meet you guys. But one condition. Stay out of trouble until I get back, all right?"

———

Dez MANAGED to track Bulldog down on the phone, and his friend was waiting at The Hub as promised when they arrived.

"You're quick," Dez said, standing just inside the entryway to the building with Bulldog and Sully.

Bulldog shrugged. "I was in the area."

"Listen, I need to head home for a bit, so I'm leaving Sully with you. Look after him, all right?"

"Come on, Dez," Sully grumbled.

"Shut up. After that stunt last night, you get no leeway with me for a while."

Sully rolled his eyes, but Dez's attention was already back on Bulldog. "I'm serious. He doesn't leave your sight. We're on top of something here, which Sully can explain to you right away. I don't want him on this by himself."

"I'm on the job, Chief," Bulldog said with a mock salute.

"I mean it, Bulldog."

"I'll watch your kid brother, all right? Chill out and go look after your kid. Jeezus."

Sully accepted one more pointed glare from Dez before his brother dashed back to his SUV and drove off in a mad hurry.

"I wish he'd stop treating me like a kid," Sully said as he watched the taillights disappearing from sight through the window.

"He can be a little intense."

Sully turned to Bulldog, eyebrows raised. "A little intense? I'm twenty and he treats me like I'm twelve. I mean, he just stuck me with a babysitter."

Bulldog shrugged. "Maybe he thinks you need one. I know a lot of guys far older than you who could use one." He dropped a beefy hand on Sully's shoulder. "Look, Copper can be a little over-the-top, but he's a good guy, and he cares about you. Everyone should be so lucky as to have someone like that in their life. And he's a big brother. I am too, and I couldn't protect my little sister. If I got a second chance, I'd be acting the same way right now."

Sully managed a smile, a real one this time, and Bulldog returned it with one of his own.

"So," the older man said. "What's this you need to fill me in on?"

The door opened as three people resembling drowned rats sloshed past them, leaving Sully visually searching what he could see of the building's interior. "Let's find somewhere quiet."

SULLY GAVE Bulldog a rundown of their conversations with Paul Dunsmore and Olivia Tan, leaving the part about Iris until the end. He wanted to break that bit to Bulldog a little more slowly.

The Hub had a small soup kitchen, and Sully and Bulldog found a so-far quiet table in the corner. As Sully talked, Bulldog slumped lower and lower in his seat until he was all but under the table.

"You really think Danny didn't kill her?" It was the first thing Bulldog had said since Sully started detailing the information they'd learned after dropping Bulldog off at his friend's last night.

"I really think that, yeah. And there's something else."

"God, what?"

Sully smiled his sympathy, then launched into the final reveal. "You remember I asked you if you knew this Iris girl?"

"Sparrow? Yeah."

"Iris Edwards is Danny's daughter."

Bulldog's gaze had been in his lap, but now it lifted to Sully's face. "Jesus, what?"

"Olivia Tan told us. I guess Danny lost custody quite some time ago and never got it back. I don't know anything else about her, unfortunately. Obviously, you didn't know that either."

"Do you think Bree knew?"

"It would explain why she seems so desperate to find her," Sully said. "I mean, Sparrow isn't her daughter, but she's Danny's so I guess there's some kind of bond there. They knew each other through the street worker program, you said. Breanna must have discovered who she was. I was hoping someone here might be able to help us. I mean, the program your sister worked with is based out of here, isn't it?"

"Yeah," Bulldog said. The word was no more than a whisper, barely a reply.

"You okay, man?"

"So I've got a little niece, and she needs my help?"

"I think so, yeah. Do you know who we could start asking?"

Something in Bulldog's face changed, desolation giving way to determination as he sat up straight in his chair. "I've got some ideas. Follow me."

Bulldog led them through The Hub, easing people out of the way as they moved. The soup kitchen tables were filling rapidly even though meal service wouldn't begin for hours. The front entry was packed, and the program spaces were starting to flood with people who likely had no affiliation with any of the programs offered.

"This is when they should be doing their municipal homeless count," Bulldog said. "Nothing brings people together like a pounding rain and risk of flood."

He led Sully through the door to the Street Worker Exit Strategy, then to one of two offices that lined the small reception area.
One of the office doors, Sully noted, was closed. Its nameplate
read Breanna Bird and the surface of the door had become a
makeshift shrine with art, flowers and other offerings taped there.

The other office was open, and a woman behind the desk
looked up as Sully and Bulldog entered.

"Billy," she said, standing and offering a hand, her face immediately reading sympathy and sorrow. "How are you?"

"Well as can be expected, Myra. How are you?"

"About the same. Still miss Bree like you wouldn't believe."
Her eyes moved to Sully, and Bulldog introduced them. "Myra
Shingoose, Sully Gray. Sully's a friend, works down at the Black
Fox. He gives me a bed some nights."

Myra's responding smile, while still tinged with grief, was a
warm one; so too was her handshake as Bulldog continued the
introduction.

"Myra runs the program and sits on the board for The Hub
overall," he said. "She was Bree's boss."

"And friend," Myra added. A tear slipped from her right eye
and started down her cheek, and Myra showed surprise as she
swiped it away. "I'm sorry. I cry so much lately, sometimes I don't
even realize I'm doing it." She waved to a couple of chairs in her
office, newer and more comfortable-looking than the ones in the
Legal Aid office. But then, The Hub hadn't really been around all
that long, had only been set up once various levels of government
were forced to recognize the sheer weight of the growing poverty
problem in KR. Like any financial slump, the wealthiest had
managed to avoid the full brunt, which fell first and heaviest on
the frontline—the workers put out of a job, the would-be workers
now struggling to find employment, and those who couldn't work
who relied on stretched government funding. Meanwhile, the
fattest cats in the city had managed to conceal their wealth in out-
of-country bank accounts that rendered it untouchable, then

proclaimed themselves just as hard-done-by as their remaining overworked employees.

Sully had plenty of opinions about the rich and few of them were positive.

"What is it I can help you with?" Myra asked, sitting behind her desk.

Sully left it to Bulldog to explain, and the older man waited a moment until Myra had plucked a tissue from a box on the desk and given her nose a gentle blow.

"My buddy Sully here recently got some information that Danny might not be the guy who killed Bree," Bulldog said.

Myra's expression read stunned. "But everyone says he admitted doing it."

"It's a bit weird, I guess, but Sully—"

Sully cut in before Bulldog revealed more than Sully was prepared to divulge about himself to this relative stranger. "I can't say who it was who told me. But I was told the man who murdered Breanna was actually a white guy. I don't have any real description but that he's about medium build and has a tattoo on his inner right forearm of a lit black candle dripping wax. I'm wondering if you know of anyone with that kind of tattoo."

Myra appeared to be giving it some thought when they were interrupted by a voice from behind them.

"I know of someone."

Sully and Bulldog turned to see a man in his early twenties standing in the doorway, bearded with long, dyed black hair pulled back into a hairnet and his clothing covered by a stained apron.

Myra paused for a brief introduction. "Zane Mazur, our soup kitchen manager." Then to Zane, "Who?"

"His name's Ken Barwell. Pardon my French, but he's a real asshole. Most of the girls here know to stay away from him. Bad date, they say."

Sully sensed movement out of the corner of his eye and fought to keep from looking directly at Breanna, who had just appeared next to Myra's desk.

"Do you happen to know where he lives?" Sully asked.

Bulldog cleared his throat and Sully sensed it was intended as a warning to him: not without Dez. Even so, it didn't hurt to get the information now so they were ready to go later.

"I don't, but I know one of the girls here went home with him once. She ended up in counselling for months."

"I know who you mean, Zane," Myra said. "I'll talk to her, see if I can get that information."

"Can I ask about something else?" Sully said. "Iris Edwards. Was she a client here?"

"Was?" Myra said. "She still is."

"When did you last see her?"

"Two days ago at our last group session. Why?"

"Has anyone seen her since? I'm hoping to talk to her."

Myra looked to Zane. "The two of you are friends, I think. Have you heard from Sparrow?"

Zane wasn't so ready with his answer this time, focusing in on Sully through narrowed eyes. "Why do you need to know?"

"I think she's in trouble. I'm thinking it's possible she went to Barwell's."

Zane's expression turned dark. "Like I said, most girls know to stay away from him. I wish I could say the same about Sparrow." Sully guessed he'd passed whatever test Zane had in mind when the kitchen manager continued talking. "I haven't heard from her since that last day she was here. She usually stays at a house some of the girls rent down on Fifteenth. I asked one of the other girls there, and she said Sparrow hasn't been around and no one's really seen her."

The shock was clear in Myra's voice. "Why didn't anyone tell me?"

"No one was freaking out about it yet. Sparrow started using again recently, and it's not exactly unusual for people to disappear for a few days while on a binge."

"I was worried about that," Myra said. She turned to Sully and Bulldog. "She hasn't really been around much the past month and has only been turning up for some of her sessions. She's seemed off to me. I tried to ask about it but she brushed me off, said everything was fine. Silly girl."

Something in her eyes suggested something had clicked in. "You don't think it could have something to do with Bree, do you? I mean, Barwell's connected and he likes the girls, if you know what I mean. You really think she might have gone there with him?"

Sully met Bulldog's eye a moment before returning attention to Myra. "It would probably be a good idea for you to get us that address as soon as possible."

"Zane?" Myra asked. "Is Abby around?"

"Yeah, I've seen her. Want me to ask her for the address?"

"If you don't mind, thank you. She's more likely to trust you with it than me."

Zane tapped Sully's shoulder. "You want to join me? I can introduce you if you want. She might know more than just the address, and might share if she thinks she can trust you."

Bulldog snagged Sully's wrist as he tried to move past. "Don't you go anywhere important without getting me first, got it?"

Sully held back the sigh. If it wasn't bad enough having Dez pulling the big brother thing at every turn, he now had to contend with Bulldog acting as an effective and equally frustrating stand-in. "Yeah, okay. Got it."

Sully followed Zane at a brisk pace down the hall and through a door. There, they crossed another hall and passed through into the currently empty kitchen area. Sully was starting to wonder why he was getting the full tour until Zane answered that question for him, shoving him back against the wall and holding him there by the collar of his jacket.

"Why are you looking for Sparrow? What do you want with her?"

"Whoa, chill out," Sully said, holding up his hands in a show of peace. "I think she might be in trouble, and I'm trying to help. That's all."

Zane didn't look wholly satisfied but released Sully anyway. "She doesn't need your help. She's got me."

"But you said you don't know where she is."

"I don't. Yet. I'm working on it."

"Just a question, man, but what's your stake in this, anyway?"

"This place has been helping to put me through university for almost three years, and I've been volunteering here for five. You don't work here and not get to know people, all right? They're not just clients to me, or mouths to feed. Some of them are friends." He backed away from Sully and leaned against the kitchen island, rubbing his face in a hand. When he looked back up, he appeared to have aged several years. "Look, you must know living around here that the girls face a lot of safety issues when working. And it's not as easy as just quitting and going straight. The centre takes a holistic approach, and the first thing is treating their addictions and past traumas so they can leave behind all the other negative things about the life. It's not unusual for the girls here to continue working while they're in programming. Some work for pimps or gangs, but not all. The ones who work for themselves don't have anyone at their backs when they're on a job, no guy to step in and act as muscle if things go bad. So some of them ask me to go with them when they're meeting a john they don't know or don't trust. I introduce myself to the guy first and say I'll be waiting outside. I guess I must come off intimidating enough because none of the girls I've escorted have come out with so much as a scratch they didn't personally allow."

"What about Sparrow? Did you help her the same way?"

"I offered. But she's young and, I hate to say, a little stupid still. The life sucks naivety out of most people on the street within days. She's different. She's been lucky so far, I guess. Or was. Listen, I want to find her as badly as you do. She's a good kid, has a good heart. She's messed up, sure, but who the hell isn't? The fact is, it hasn't changed who she is, and that's a beautiful thing to see around here. I'm hoping to keep it that way."

"Me, too. Listen, I really need to get moving on this. Any chance you can find Abby for that address?"

"No need. I know where Barwell lives."

"So why'd you say—"

"I wanted to talk to you alone, find out what the hell you were up to. Sorry. As you can no doubt tell, I'm a little protective of the girls and a lot suspicious of strangers. Barwell lives at 1254 Mitchenson. It's a pretty typical house for Riverview, but he's got security cameras up, so you'll be able to pick it out easily enough. Normally I'd go with you, but I've got a crapload of prep to do here, and it looks like you've got Bulldog at your back. Be careful though. Everyone knows Barwell runs his guns and drugs out of that place. He won't take kindly to strangers turning up on his doorstep."

"I'll keep that in mind, thanks."

"You'd better," Zane said. "If you don't, you can forget about finding Sparrow. Kenton Barwell will be the last face you'll ever see."

9

"WE SHOULDN'T DO THIS," Bulldog said, huffing through a jog. "Not without Dez."

"I tried calling him," Sully said. "I'm not getting through. Maybe his phone's dead."

"Copper's phone is never dead. Did you try his work cell? That one's always on."

Sully and Bulldog ran until they reached the nearest bus shelter, then ducked inside with the three other people who'd had the same idea.

Make that four. Breanna was back, standing in the corner next to an unsuspecting man holding a bag from the nearby drug store. The man ducked, barely avoiding a beak-on-head collision with a small brown sparrow that dove inside the shelter. It flapped to the ground, alighting at Breanna's feet where it shook the rain from its body.

Sully hadn't been able to get a message to Dez yet, but Breanna was still working at getting her own through to Sully.

He pulled his phone from his sodden hoodie pocket, grateful for the sandwich bag Myra had given him to keep it safe from the rain.

It occurred to him this wasn't a conversation he should be

having around other people, so he opted to text both his brother's phones instead. *With Bulldog. Need to check a lead at Ken B's. 1254 Mitchenson.*

Sully estimated it was about a twenty-minute walk to that address, ten if they really hoofed it and cut through some yards. They could chop the time down by bus, though, and he was checking the city transit website for the right route when his phone rang in his hand. Dez's face showed on the call display, a big, goofy grin and a thumbs-up. Chances were that wasn't the expression he was wearing right now.

Sully looked around for somewhere quiet to talk, and was saved by an approaching bus that emptied the bus shelter. He and Bulldog took the bench inside while Sully reluctantly answered.

"Hey, Dez."

"What the hell are you doing? Where are you?"

"Bus shelter down the street from The Hub."

"Stay there. I'm coming to get you. I just dropped Kayleigh off with Mom."

"You're at least half an hour away."

"What's your point? I mean it, Sully. You plant your ass and you keep it that way, you hear me? Don't you go near Barwell's. He dangerous."

"I know he is. That's the problem. We think there's a chance Sparrow went there and he's known as a rough date. If she's in trouble, we might not have a lot of time to waste. She's been missing two days already."

"If it's been two days, I doubt you need to worry about wasting time. Everything's probably been decided for us."

"But it could be they've just been using together and nothing worse has happened yet."

"Barwell doesn't use. He just sells. He's a commercial dealer, in it for the money. He's got a lot to lose, Sully, and he's not going to put up with some kid turning up on his doorstep asking questions."

Sully bristled, bottoming out on his usually sky-high patience.

Dez was only three years older, but sometimes he acted like a decade separated them. When they'd been younger, it had been reassuring to have Dez's hulking presence at his side as a threat to would-be bullies. Sully had since grown his own two feet, but it was pretty hard to stand on them when his big brother insisted on pushing him back down. "Well, everything's cool then, Dez, because as it happens, I'm not a kid."

He clicked the button to end the call, then silenced the phone before putting it back into the plastic bag and stuffing it with some heated force back into the confines of his hoodie pocket.

"We need a Number 17," Sully said.

"Whoa, reign it in there, cowboy," Bulldog said. "What is it you think we're doing exactly?"

"We're heading to Barwell's."

"We can't. Not without Copper."

"He's half an hour away on a good day. Traffic's crawling and streets are flooding right now, so you can probably add another fifteen minutes to half an hour to that. Then we need to get to Barwell's from here, which is another ten minutes by car. If Sparrow's there and she's in trouble, we could be wasting some serious time."

Bulldog was scanning the pavement, jowls hanging lower than usual as his face clouded with doubt. "I don't know. I promised your brother …."

"Breanna's here, Bulldog. Maybe that means we're getting close to something."

Or she was here. As Sully turned to look, he spotted her not in the corner of the shelter but back at the door to The Hub at the end of the block.

No matter. They had a lead now and the sooner they figured this out, the quicker he could get the unsettling image of the murdered woman out of his life.

"Bree's here?"

"She was a second ago."

Bulldog blew out a breath. "I'm a lover not a fighter, Sully. You know that. But if my niece needs me, I'll try to change my ways."

Bulldog's phone was ringing now and the gap in time suggested Sully likely had two or three missed calls from Dez. Bulldog pulled the phone out and checked the screen.

"Whoosh. It's your brother." He met Sully's eye for a moment and then flicked the ringer to silent before stuffing the bagged phone back into the pocket of his wet jeans. "Number 17, you say?"

THE BUS RIDE wasn't much quicker than the walk would have been, it turned out—particularly since they missed the right stop and ended up having to jog back three blocks.

There was nothing extraordinary about 1254 Mitchenson Avenue, nothing but a nondescript house sitting on a xeriscaped front yard that was bleeding weeds. The house looked like every other one on the block—until you looked closer.

A well-timed break in the heavy rain revealed this residence had a solid steel front door and what looked to be a decent deadbolt system. Two visible basement windows were made impassable by bars. And then, as Zane Mazur had described, there was the security camera mounted at the corner of the house, aimed at the front door.

"Why would someone like that want to record people coming and going?" Sully asked. "Wouldn't that be bad for business?"

"Probably not hooked up to a recording device," Bulldog said. "It's probably just so he can check who's come calling before he answers the door."

With the front door looking less like a means of entry, Sully and Bulldog circled the block until they reached the back alley, counting houses until they got to the one they knew to be the back of 1254.

Here, there was an old one-car garage and an unmarked forest green delivery van parked next to it. The backyard didn't contain anything of a lawn either, although it had a large back deck and patio area that meant neighbours didn't feel so put upon by the weeds as to start calling City Hall demanding sanctions. The layout was suggestive of a smart man; the last thing a trafficker wanted was the wrong sort of attention, and an experienced trafficker knew how to avoid it.

"See any cameras?" Sully asked.

"I can't make out the back of the house from here," Bulldog said. "Rain's coming too hard."

Sully, hunched against the weather with hands stuffed deep in the pockets of his jeans, turned to Bulldog. "Between the two of us, I'm thinking I look more the type to be looking to buy."

"I don't think people come here for street-level purchases," Bulldog said. "He's a wholesaler. Just sells to gangsters and they hand off to their dealers who make the trades."

"So what other excuse do we have to go in there?"

Bulldog shrugged. "Beats me. Looking for a lost dog?"

Sully pulled a hand from his pocket long enough to give Bulldog a shove. "Look, I'm going to try it. Stay here and—"

"I don't think you should be going in there by yourself."

"Listen to me. I need you to stay here so that in case I don't come out right away you can call Dez. He'll get someone here if he's still out of range."

"I think I should go in."

"No offence, Bulldog, but you're how old now?"

"Thirty-nine."

"And holding?"

"Fuck you. So I'm forty-four. What's your point?"

"Nothing, other than the fact you're a bit old to be looking to make a buy like this."

Bulldog's face slumped, the look of defeat. "You got cash on you? He's going to want to know you're serious."

"I get paid in cash, and payday was last week. I've got plenty left in the wallet."

Bulldog's face broke into a gradual grin. "Wanna scrap this idea and buy us a round?"

"Bulldog."

"I'm just kidding. Jesus. I don't like this, Sully. We don't even know she's in there, and this guy might be the one who killed Bree. And Copper's gonna send me to join her if I let anything happen to you."

"Look, you're not letting anything happen to me. I'm doing this myself, all right? My choice. Do us all a favour. Call Dez and tell him we decided not to talk to Barwell."

"Lie to him, you mean."

"It's for his own good. If he thinks he can't get to us in time, he'll call in the troops. Next thing is he'll be facing internal investigation for digging into someone else's case without clearing it first. After you talk to him, wait here and give me ten minutes. If I'm not out, call Dez back and break the news."

"I'll give you five."

It sounded like a fair compromise and, as Sully started through the backyard toward the equally solid-looking back door, he figured he would have been satisfied with a two-minute cutoff. A lot could happen in five. By the time police arrived, he could be dead and gutted with Kenton Barwell making soup out of his innards.

As he approached the rear door, Sully forced himself not to take a reassuring glance back at Bulldog, not wanting to reveal the other man given the very real possibility Kenton was watching via CCTV. Instead, he kept his eyes focused forward on the steel door as he searched for a doorbell. He came up empty, but it appeared his presence had been noted as the door was yanked open in front of him.

The bald, bearded man on the other side was a couple inches shorter than Sully's six-foot frame, but easily made up for his lesser height with the solid-looking, nickel-plated revolver in his hand. Sully took an involuntary step back as he eyed the barrel levelled at his gut.

"What the hell do you want?" The man's voice was every bit as cold and hard as the gun in his hand, and the eyes just as soulless.

Sully fought to push his brain and his gaze past those eyes and the threat of the gun but found Kenton's arms concealed beneath the long sleeves of a sweatshirt. No way to get a look at any tattoos he might have there.

"Uh …."

"I asked you a question."

"I was told I might be able to buy some coke here."

The response took the situation from bad to worse as Kenton's free hand came out and balled into the front of Sully's hoodie, yanking him in and shoving him back against the wall. Sully winced as what was likely a set of light switches dug into his skin while Kenton kicked the door shut beside them.

Sully was trying to push away from the wall when the gun, its barrel brought to press up against the bottom of his chin with some force, had him changing his mind.

"You're a fucking narc," Kenton said, his voice unnervingly calm and close enough to Sully's ear that he could feel the older man's breath. "Aren't you."

It wasn't a question, but it merited a response and a quick one.

"No, I'm not. I swear. I'm looking for some coke. That's all."

"I don't fucking deal and you don't use. I know a coke-head when I see one. Why don't you tell me what you're really doing here."

"Let me go, and we can talk about it."

"No, I think we're going to have this conversation right here. Start talking or I'm going to put a couple new holes in your head and call this in as a home invasion."

There was no way Sully could cop to the truth. If Sparrow really was being held against her will here—or worse, had Kenton already killed her—Sully would wind up buried next to her pretty damn fast.

"I'm looking to get into the trade," Sully said. "I know people who know people and I heard you're the guy to talk to."

"You heard wrong," Kenton said. Then icily, "Dead wrong."

"But you're a legend on the street."

A lesser man might have bowed to the praise. Kenton Barwell was not a lesser man, and neither his gun nor his grip on Sully wavered.

"Who have you been talking to?"

Damn. "I'm not supposed to say."

"Well, you'd better reconsider or you won't be saying anything to anyone ever again. I had some damned little whore rip me off not so long ago. I've got no more patience for bullshit, and you stink of it."

A rap on the door provided Sully with a moment to think, although forming a coherent thought was difficult given the unrelenting press of the gun.

"Who the fuck you bring with you?" Kenton asked.

"I came alone," Sully said.

"Bullshit. No one comes here alone."

"I swear, man. I don't know."

Kenton pulled back with his gun hand just enough so he could look Sully in the eye. "No, *I* swear. If I answer that door and I get even the tiniest whiff of a setup, I'm putting a bullet in both of you. You got me?"

Sully managed a nod and hoped for the best as Kenton released his hoodie to allow him to ease the door open a crack. The movement allowed Sully a glimpse down at Kenton's arms, the sleeves having ridden up to mid-forearm with position and movement. Both arms were covered in tattoos, and old ones at that. Definitely no evidence he'd been limited to just one tattoo a month ago when Breanna was killed. What was more, Sully was able to pick out the candle dyed into the man's skin. It was on the outer left forearm, not the inner right.

All of this, and they weren't even dealing with the right man. Kenton Barwell hadn't killed Breanna.

But give him a couple more minutes and it was likely he'd be responsible for a murder nonetheless.

Kenton's voice was hard as he answered the door. "What?"

Sully couldn't turn his head to look, but he recognized Bull-dog's voice. "Uh, hey there. I'm looking for my dog."

There was a smile in Kenton's voice when it next came, but whatever he found amusing was known only to the man himself. "You're in luck. I think I've got your puppy right here. Come on in and get him."

Bulldog's voice was closer when Sully next heard it. "What, that guy? I'm talking about a dog, man. A yapping little cocker spaniel named Jones. You see a dog like that anywhere?"

Bulldog's voice was solid and unfazed, the tone of a man who'd seen it all, survived to tell the tale and had emerged all the more jaded for it. There was nothing to suggest he was troubled by the fact the man he was addressing had a guy up against the wall with a revolver jammed under his jaw.

"Look, I've got a photo in my pocket," Bulldog said. "Let me get it."

"Keep your hands where I can see them."

"Here's the thing, man," Bulldog said. "It was a rough night. I let the dog out for a piss, and the little bastard took off and didn't come back. My old lady gets home later today, and if she finds out I'm back on the bottle and lost her dog, she's gonna bust my balls."

"That's your problem, not mine." Were he not so preoccupied by the handgun, Sully would have been amazed by Kenton's response—an indication he'd bought into Bulldog's story. "Get the hell out of here."

But Bulldog didn't move.

"You got a problem?" Kenton asked him.

"Maybe you should let the kid go."

"The kid's not your problem."

Out of the corner of his eye, Sully saw Bulldog shrug, noncommittal as ever. "Just looks to me like he's been out of diapers all of three years. Bit young to have his face blown off."

From somewhere in the distance came the sound of sirens, and Sully found himself wondering if Bulldog had failed to reach Dez —or worse, had been on the phone with him when Sully had been dragged inside the house.

Kenton looked from Bulldog to Sully and back again. "Look me in the eye and tell me this punk's not your boy."

Bulldog laughed. "Do I look like I'd be hanging with some dumb-ass white boy who looks like he's probably trying to deal his way through college?"

"Are those cops coming here?"

"How the fuck should I know? I'm looking for a damn dog. Maybe the kid's a narc."

"Fuck. I knew it. I fucking knew it!"

Bulldog took a step closer, allowing him to keep his voice low and conspiratorial as he addressed Kenton. "I were you, I'd let the kid go and start flushing whatever shit you've got here. If the cops are coming 'cause of him, better for you he's found intact. And if he's just a punk, I'm thinking he's not gonna want mommy and daddy knowing he was here, so he'll keep the last few minutes to himself. Am I right, junior?"

Sully nodded.

"Fuck," Kenton muttered. It took him a few more seconds' thought before he decided Bulldog was making some sense, and he let Sully go with a solid glare. "I ever catch you here again, we won't be having a conversation, you got me?"

Sully didn't have a chance to reply, Kenton turning and rushing into the house as Bulldog tugged Sully toward the door.

"Let's go," Bulldog said.

Sully didn't argue, saving his questions for the jog through the yard and down the alley.

"Thanks, man."

"Forget it," Bulldog said. "And take a note. Dog story worked."

"Are those cars coming here?"

"Not that I know of. I think it must have been a fluke."

"So Dez wasn't going to call anyone in to check on us?"

"I managed to convince him we weren't so stupid as to check out Barwell on our own. He wanted to talk to you, but I told him you had a sulk on and weren't in the talkative mood. I doubt that's going to hold him for long. If I were you, I'd give him a call."

The sirens had stopped somewhere in the distance, proving Bulldog right. They had been lucky, that was all.

"Did we get anything out of this?" Bulldog asked.

"Did you see his arms?"

"Nope. As it happened, my eyes were kind of narrowed in on that .357."

"Barwell doesn't fit, Bulldog. His arms are covered in tattoos and the candle is in the wrong spot."

"So all that, and this wasn't even the right guy?"

"Yeah, looks that way."

"Ordinarily, I'd be put out, but I have to say I'm thrilled Sparrow's not in there with him."

"Me too," Sully said. "But he said something interesting, something about a 'little whore' having ripped him off."

"Maybe he meant that Abby girl."

"I don't think so. The way he said it made it sound like the girl got what she wanted and got out. We were told he hurt Abby. Given what just happened, I'd say if he caught someone stealing, they wouldn't get the chance ever again. Abby wouldn't be hurt, she'd be dead."

"So you think he meant Sparrow?" Bulldog asked. "If she ripped him off, that's reason right there for him to want to find her and kill her. Rep like he's got, he can't afford to let word get around he's soft on that sort of thing. Maybe he got to her already."

"Maybe," Sully said. "But that still leaves us with the guy Breanna's been showing me, and it's definitely not Barwell. Question is, if it wasn't Kenton Barwell who Breanna showed me, then who was it?"

Sully had heard the expression about deafening silence before, but it wasn't until this moment he really understood it.

Dez had picked them up a few minutes ago and had yet to say a word. The atmosphere thickened with all the things that hadn't yet been spoken and some of the things that probably wouldn't.

It wasn't clear to Sully whether Dez was heading anywhere in particular, given he'd avoided the thoroughfare that would have led them over to Gladstone. And while they were still in the Riverview neighbourhood, Dez had taken them past the streets that led to the Black Fox, The Hub and to the place where Bulldog had stayed last night.

Sully pulled out his phone, meaning to check the time, but found his gaze diverted by the notification of missed calls from Dez. Seven in total.

Sully redirected his gaze from the phone's screen to the side of his brother's head, finding the jaw just as tension-set as it had been when Dez first picked them up a few blocks from Kenton Barwell's.

"Dez—"

"Don't talk to me."

"Look, I'm—"

"Shut up, Sullivan."

Sully faced the windshield, knowing better than to attempt further conversation. It wasn't the "shut up" that had done it; it was the use of his entire first name, one Dez didn't pronounce in full unless he was making a formal introduction or beyond pissed off. The use of the name Sullivan was just one step below a punch in the face as far as the two of them went.

And there was still a very real possibility that punch was on its way once Dez pulled the SUV over. Maybe Dez had come to the same realization and wanted to avoid it, because he chose that moment to break his silence.

"You can be a real selfish dick, you know that? You think I told you to stay away from Barwell's because I was excited to drop in on the guy myself? And don't try to lie to me and tell me you didn't go there. The two of you weren't just out for a leisurely stroll in a torrential downpour when you happened to end up a few blocks from his house. So?"

This sounded like a trick question. "So, what?"

"Tell me the truth. You went there, right?"

There was no right answer, except that Sully had never been able or willing to lie to Dez's face. There were some truths he just simply hadn't spoken out loud, but always ones Dez hadn't realized needed exploring. There was a difference between holding one's tongue and using it to lie, and it was a line Sully had never wanted to cross with his family.

Sully risked a glance back at Bulldog, knowing the movement itself would give them away. Bulldog met him with a frown and a shrug, and Sully returned his attention to Dez.

Dez who was now steaming like the kitchen of an Italian restaurant at dinner hour.

"Yeah, we went there," Sully said, the words emerging so quietly even he had trouble hearing them.

Dez slammed on the brakes, sending up a spray of water

either side. For a moment, he didn't speak, white knuckles gripping the steering wheel and clenched jaw doing all the talking for him.

It didn't last long. The Braddocks weren't naturally violent, but they could yell with the best of them, allowing Dez's natural booming voice an outlet to exhibit itself to its fullest. And Sully sat through it as he was verbally pummelled, knowing his brother had been right to warn them against going to Kenton Barwell's and right to worry. Had it not been for Bulldog, Sully fully expected he would be dead rather than sitting here, suffering through the impact of Dez's explosion.

It had to happen eventually, that Dez would turn his attention to Bulldog. "And you. How the hell could you let him go to Barwell's?"

"Let me?" Sully cut in. His head spun with all the things he wanted to say, but a sudden fury he barely recognized as his own prevented him from stringing together any one of those thoughts into an actual sentence. All he managed were three words. "Fuck you, Desmond."

He supposed it was down to shock that Dez didn't make a grab for him when Sully jumped out of the SUV and started toward Riverview Park, just a block or so back and to the north. He didn't expect he'd get far, and he was right, Dez cutting him off before he'd even had a chance to make it much past the vehicle.

"Get back in the car," Dez said.

"No."

Sully expected a threat that failure to obey would result in Dez's putting his younger brother bodily in the vehicle, so he was surprised by the response that followed hard on the heels of a deep breath.

"Please, Sully. Get back in the car."

The plea was there, not just in words but in Dez's eyes, and it occurred to Sully they had entered unfamiliar territory. They'd fought from time to time, of course, as all brothers did. But never about anything serious, and never in any way that threatened to upset the natural flow they'd established years ago. Dez was older and had a past and a personality that lent themselves to protecting others, especially his younger brother—a fact he'd been plenty prepared to prove over the years. Sully, on the other hand, had been small and shy as a kid—in many ways, still was—and he'd happily nestled in under Dez's wing. Most of the time, he was still fine with it, was laid back enough and appreciative enough to allow his big brother's mother-henning to go unchecked.

But they'd hit a roadblock here somewhere, one Sully expected neither of them had seen coming. And beyond that, a fork lay in the road. He knew a lot of siblings who'd separated at that fork, who'd taken different paths and only came together once in a while —usually at weddings, funerals and tension-filled Christmas dinners. For Sully—and for Dez, judging by that imploring expression lingering on his face—that wasn't a route either of them wanted to take.

Sully returned to the car.

THEY ENDED up back at the Black Fox where Sully grabbed the three of them a beer.

Dez was still vibrating with tension, but he had bitten his tongue on the matter, so Sully breached the gap with the apology he knew he owed his brother.

"I'm sorry, Dez. You were right. We shouldn't have gone to Barwell's."

"Did you get anything out of it?" Dez's voice was tight, but the question in place of an "I told you so" was further proof he was trying hard.

Sully shook his head. "He's got the candle, but it's on the wrong arm. And he's got a pile of others. The arms Breanna showed me were more or less bare of other tattoos." He took a swig of his beer before daring to utter the next words. "I've been thinking. Maybe I need to go back to the house where she died, see if I can get a second vision of it."

"No," Dez said. "No way in hell."

"Dez—"

"There are other ways. We can start checking tattoo parlours, see if anyone's been doing tattoos like that. The ones you've seen, could you tell how old they were?"

"They've been there a while, I'd say. It was clear the colour was meant to be black, but it had faded out a bit and the edges weren't crisp."

"And were they identical, or just kind of similar?"

"I'd say identical," Sully said. "The only difference that jumped out at me was the opposite arm thing, and the other tattoos Barwell has."

"So that's somewhere to start," Dez said. He turned to Bulldog. "Any chance you could check out a few tattoo parlours for us, see if anyone's done anything like that? It could be it's just something in a book they've been doing for a bunch of people."

"No offence to your theory, but Barwell doesn't strike me as the kind of guy who gets his tattoos out of a book," Bulldog said. "And I don't know a lot of tough guys who go running to get candle tats. Not quite butterflies and unicorns, but it's sure as hell not a skull or a snake either."

"Even so, hopefully given the candles looked identical, it's the same artist. If we can find that person, we'll be a hell of a lot closer to figuring out who they worked on."

"So what about you two?" Bulldog asked.

"You're right about the candle thing," Dez said. "Not likely these two guys just pulled it out of the air. So it has to mean something. Fun part's going to be figuring out what. Luckily, there's someone I think we can ask."

Marc Echoles had the look of an aging hipster.

The man who came to the door of his office in the university's arts building had long, greyed hair tied back into a ponytail and was dressed head to toe in various shades of black.

Dez had provided a brief explanation to Sully on the way over. Marc—a professor of occult studies, among other courses—had been the complainant in a residential break-in approximately a year ago, had reported waking up to find a guy inside his house. It had been a fairly simple investigation requiring no more than a couple patrol units and a sharp eye to locate the college student dashing down the street with the intricate and expensive ceremonial dagger he'd stolen from Marc's altar. Other officers had brushed Marc off as slightly crackers; Dez had left the guy's house seriously spooked.

"I swear, he could see right into my brain," Dez had told Sully with a shiver. Now that they were standing in front of him, Sully could see what his brother had been talking about.

Marc recognized Dez immediately, reaching out with a hand and shaking a friendly greeting. But he promptly turned eyes on Sully and his mouth dropped open about an inch as he peered at the younger man through a pair of round glasses.

Marc didn't bother to wait on an introduction. "You're a seer."

Dez looked from Marc to Sully, as if trying to see what the other man had noticed. "Uh, Mr. Echoles, this is—"

"Marc, please." Still focused unnervingly on Sully, his eyes fixed on him in a way that had Sully wanting to look away but unable to.

"Right. This is my brother, Sullivan Gray."

"Different names," Marc said. He didn't wait for the usual explanation before coming up with one of his own. "Different histories. You aren't blood brothers."

"Foster," Sully said. "Dez's family took me in when I was a kid."

"But not soon enough."

"I'm sorry?"

"You've known trauma, but you've had the chance to heal. Desmond is a good and a kind man, and while he's suffered through tragedy, he's lived a good life with a stable, loving family. As far as you're concerned, they saved you. Not just from the outside world, but from the man you could have become."

Sully didn't have to see Dez's expression to know just how uncomfortable his brother had to be right now. Sully was feeling plenty of his own discomfort at this inexplicable intrusion into his soul. But where the unease had bred something approaching fear in Dez, Sully found he was fascinated.

"How do you know all that?"

"I'm a seer too," Marc said. "I'll explain if you have the time, but I sense the two of you are on something of a mission." He returned his gaze to Dez, a shift that appeared to take some effort as he broke the connection with Sully. "What is it you need to ask me?"

Dez's eyes were still a little round, and he'd lost a shade of colour beneath the smattering of freckles, suggesting Sully would be taking pointe in this conversation.

"We're looking for someone," Sully said. "A man. I don't have anything of a description other than that he's a Caucasian and he's got a tattoo on his inner right forearm. The tattoo is probably key to this, but we're struggling to find someone with anything matching the description."

"I take it there's an occult connection or you wouldn't be here," Marc said.

"It's a candle," Sully said. "A black candle. Lit and dripping wax. We're hoping you might be able to tell us something about the meaning."

"I see," Marc said. "And what is it this tattooed man has allegedly done?"

Dez finally found his tongue. "He killed a woman."

This time, Marc's eyes were the ones to widen, although he regained his composure quickly. "That's unfortunate."

"Yeah," Dez said. "So could we ask about the symbology?"

"Of course I would be pleased to answer any questions you have," Marc said. "But I feel I should tell you something first. Or, rather, show you."

And he pulled up the sleeve of his black turtleneck to reveal on his right, inner forearm a dripping, lit black candle.

11

DEZ TRIED NOT to stare at the tattoo. Sully was doing a good job of that already.

Sully didn't have to say it out loud, the expression on his face and the fading colour in his cheeks telling Dez this was the tattoo he'd been shown last night.

Dez considered confronting Marc right there, but in the few seconds he had before the silence became awkward, he decided that wasn't the right way to go. Not yet anyway.

He came down in favour of playing it cool, asking questions while Marc was more likely to remain cooperative. It was just as likely he'd put up some smokescreens to try to throw them off his trail, but he'd do the same thing if confronted with an accusation.

"What does it signify?" Dez asked.

"It signifies stupidity," Marc said. He waved an arm toward his office and a pair of chairs this side of his desk. "Why don't you come in and we can discuss it? I'm just instructing a summer class right now, and I'm done teaching for the day. I should be marking papers, but I could use a break."

Dez led the way in, taking one of the chairs and watching Sully as he lowered himself into the other. Sully was still pale and quiet and it was clear to Dez he'd withdrawn somewhere within himself, was probably envisioning what he'd seen and performing the mental comparisons to be certain of what they were dealing with here.

Dez hated the idea of ghosts and wasn't afraid to admit to his fear. But criminals he understood. He could deal with that, and so he did, taking the lead on this conversation as Marc slid into a beat-up desk chair across a desktop littered with stacks of books and essays.

Marc didn't wait for further questions, simply picking up the narrative he'd started with that self-deprecating comment and matching smile a minute ago.

"I'm sure you recall I'm a practicing Wiccan," Marc said. "I spent much of my adult life practicing with my life partner, just the two of us. But when she passed away seven years ago, I temporarily let go of my beliefs. I went into a very dark place, and I can see now the mistakes I made as a result. After a few months of withdrawing from the world and sitting around stewing in my depression, I decided a change might be in order. I wanted to reconnect with my faith, but I couldn't face the idea of practicing at home, alone, where Mariel and I devoted so much time. So, for the first time in my life, I sought out a coven. It was a terrible mistake, one I've regretted since."

Dez nodded toward Marc's right arm, once again concealed beneath his black sleeve. "And I take it this coven has something to do with the tattoo."

"You take it correctly, Desmond. I should ask, I may call you Desmond?"

"No problem."

Marc nodded with a small smile and continued. "Keep in mind, the coven already existed before I came to it. Those practicing within it called it the Black Candle."

"No offence, but didn't that put you off?"

"Those who don't understand Wicca or candle magic mistakenly believe black candles are connected with the dark side of the craft. They actually signify the exact opposite—a protection against darkness. I was looking for that in my life at the time, and I believed the others shared my views. I was wrong. Now, they understood the basics of Wiccan practice well enough and the ceremonies were as I remembered, with a few tweaks here and there. And most of them were good people, and accepted me and supported me, and so I stayed for a few years. I even got the tattoo. Coven members all have one, a rite of passage and communion I didn't quite understand but accepted nonetheless. At that point, I saw no harm in it."

"But you do now."

"I said *most* of the members were good people. I should explain that I have a rather unusual talent that allows me to see a person's aura. From the time I was a young boy, I could see bright colours emanating from most of the people I met. In you for instance, Desmond, I see strong golds. This tells me you are guided by divine good, that you possess an inner wisdom. I also see greens that suggest to me you are a loving, social person, although some muddier blues tell me you have some fears you have yet to face. Sullivan possesses some remarkably bright royal blues, whites and indigos that show his third eye is open and seeing, that he is spiritual and in touch with higher dimensions."

Dez shifted in his chair; Marc chuckled.

"I see one of the areas you struggle with is acceptance of this world beyond your five senses. I expect Sullivan has been placed within your life to teach you about that world so you might find a way through your fears. In turn, you are his protector and an earth guide to him."

Dez shifted again, tried to disguise the unintentional show of discomfort by crossing an ankle over his knee. "You were talking about the coven."

Marc allowed one more amused smile, but it drifted away as he continued. "There were a few members who were surrounded by dark colours—blacks, muddy greys and darker, non-earth tone browns. It was clear they were bent under the weight of grief, pressure or greed, or something else that had stolen their light.

But most people suffering through these types of challenges still retain the brighter colours that identify the goodness within them. These men seemed to have little of that colour left. That's how I know they were no longer what I would call good men."

"Who were they?"

"You have to understand, Desmond, Wicca is not a widely accepted religion. Those who practice are subject to judgment and ridicule, and sometimes outright hate and even violence. I have no shame in my choice of religious path or my practices and I have chosen to live openly. Many haven't. The coven operates under a code of silence that dictates we are not to reveal the identities of other members. Although I no longer practice with them, I hold to that pledge."

"But you can confirm that anyone with that black candle tattoo is a member?"

"Or was in the past. I believe I am safe in confirming that for you. The tattoo artist who does the work is a member of the coven. I can't imagine she'd ink anyone outside the circle with the candle. It's intended to be unique to the group."

"And since you're no longer a member, there was no push to have you get the tattoo removed?" Dez asked.

Marc quirked up a corner of his mouth. "I know what you're getting at, and no. The Black Candle is a coven, not a street gang. One can come and go at will. There was no beatdown for me and no threat to forcefully remove my tattoo if I didn't do it myself. It's there for life if I want it."

"Why'd you leave, anyway?" Dez asked. "Was it just because of those members?"

"Not wholly, no. There was a tragedy that occurred within the circle a little over a year ago. I was still grieving my partner's loss at the time and I couldn't bear the additional hurt, particularly because the new loss darkened so many souls within the coven. People changed after that. It was as if their light had been stolen and I was surrounded by darkness when I was there. After two meetings, I couldn't take it anymore so I stopped going."

"What was the name of the person who died?" Dez asked. When Marc's gaze dropped to his desktop, and he failed to provide an immediate response, Dez pushed on. "If the only reason for not identifying members is to protect them from fallout, then there shouldn't be any problem telling us this person's name. Not now. Anyway, it will just stay with us, and I think you're well aware Sully and I are the last people to judge."

Marc nodded and met Dez's eye once again. "Her name was Gabriella Aguado. She was a beautiful young woman, so full of light and life. Her death all but broke me."

Dez uncrossed his legs, allowing him to sit forward. "You said there were members of the group you didn't like. Did you ever suspect any of them of being involved in her death?"

"As far as I'm aware, no one was involved in her death. She drowned in the Kimotan River. Gabriella was beautiful, but she had some problems. I don't believe she committed suicide, but I think her decision to use chemicals to heighten her awareness led to her death. I have no doubt you could access the file at police headquarters if you wanted to know more. I'm afraid I don't know much else about it. I distanced myself from the coven following that, so anything they might have shared with each other, I wasn't privy to."

"Can I ask you one more question?" Dez asked. "Does the name Kenton Barwell mean anything to you?"

"You're asking if he was a coven member," Marc said.

"He's got a black candle tattoo on his left arm identical to yours," Dez said. "I'd assume that means something."

"Since you've seen the tattoo, you don't need my confirmation."

It was all the reply Marc offered and, as it happened, it was all Dez needed.

———

THE NEXT LOGICAL STOP, after phoning Bulldog to call off what would be a pointless search of tattoo parlours, was police head-quarters and a trip up the elevator to Administration.

Deputy Chief Flynn Braddock had the smaller of two corner offices, and Dez checked to ensure his backside was more or less dry before dropping it into one of several leather armchairs that circled a small round table in the corner. Sully went to stand at the window, the grey city barely visible through the rain-streaked eighth-floor window.

"You haven't said much since we left Echoles's office," Dez said, craning his neck to speak to Sully's back.

Sully didn't move, hands remaining stuffed deep in the pockets of his jeans. "Sometimes it's easy to forget I'm not the only freak out there."

Dez reached back, his arm plenty long enough to allow him to swat Sully none-too-gently on the backside. "Don't use that word. We've had this discussion."

"I saw the way you looked at Echoles, Dez. If you didn't know me, you'd look at me the same way. You know you would."

"Two things, man. I *do* know you, and I don't think of you or anyone else like you in that way. My fears are my hangup, not yours. I like threats I can see and do something about. And it isn't you or him or anyone living and breathing. It's the fact there's this whole world around us I know nothing about. We've all got talents, Sull. This is yours. Mine's hockey."

That got him the reaction he wanted, Sully letting loose a surprised laugh and turning his head just enough to smirk at Dez. "Hockey? Seriously? Dude, you suck."

Dez grinned back. "Point taken. But I'm damn good at kicking your ass."

He didn't get a chance to prove it as the door opened and Flynn walked in, face breaking into a wide smile when he saw his visitors. It disappeared just as quickly. "What did the two of you get into this time?"

"What makes you think we got into anything?" Dez said. "You know us better than that."

"Damn right I know you. That's why I'm worried." Flynn peered at Sully. "You're not opening the bar today, I hope. Streets down that way are full of water. Lots of places are closed and in damage control mode."

"Crap," Sully said. "I haven't been back recently to check. I'll bet the basement's flooded."

"I'll take you over there right away," Dez said. But first, they had something else they needed to deal with. "Dad, we're in the middle of something we need help with."

Flynn dropped solidly into the nearest chair. "I knew it. One of you in trouble or is this a Sully matter?"

"Sully matter" had become a sort of code in their family. "The latter," Dez said.

Sully finally drifted over to sit next to Dez, allowing him to face their father as he gave Flynn the rundown. He didn't leave anything out, even admitting to the ill-advised exploration of the abandoned house and the trip to Kenton Barwell's. Sully had to have expected the scolding, particularly over the Barwell incident, and he got it—albeit a lighter and less expletive-filled version than the one he'd earned from Dez earlier.

"Why would you do something like that? Damn it, Sully, you know better. Dez was on his way. You should have waited." He turned eyes on Dez next. "And you shouldn't have been considering going there either without at least three units at your back. Goddammit, don't the two of you go getting stupid on me. I've already lost one son. I'll be damned if I'm going to lose the other two. You're not invincible. Either of you."

"We know, Dad," Dez said. "You're right. It won't happen again. Right, Sully?"

Sully was scanning the tabletop and managed only a tight nod in response. It was obvious he was fighting emotion, but Dez knew his brother well enough to realize it wasn't over the mild tongue-lashing; it was the fact Flynn had referred to him as his son. Thirteen years had passed since Sully first came into their lives, and he still showed various levels of surprise when anyone besides Dez described him as family. To Dez, Sully was so engrained in the Braddock clan it was sometimes easy to forget he had a prior life in which he'd never really belonged—and, in at least a few cases Dez was aware of, had been told exactly that.

Dez landed a hand solidly on Sully's knee, giving his leg an affectionate shake.

"I know you can't get us a look at the Breanna Bird file as it's still an open case, but I'm wondering if there's anything we could scan in relation to Iris Edwards or Gabriella Aguado. I didn't want to start tapping into stuff in our system myself just yet, especially with regards to Iris Edwards."

"Smart move," Flynn said. Then he added with a wink, "Could be your first of the day. I'll be sure to check in with Major Crimes on the Bird matter, just to make sure they're following through on re-interviewing Danny Newton. As for the other stuff, pull up a chair and let's check the system."

Moving to Flynn's desk and his computer, they found little on Iris Edwards. She was more or less a blank at this point, other than a recent arrest for possession of cocaine after she'd been caught ripping someone off at a known party house. There were no missing person reports and nothing else to suggest anyone out there was at all worried about her. Dez knew better, of course, thanks to Sully and Bulldog.

Gabriella Aguado's file was a little more helpful, though not much.

"Her body was found in the North Kimotan, just east of the rapids," Flynn said. "It was believed she died a number of days before that. There were some unanswered questions due to the level of water-related decomposition, but the coroner ruled her death an accident upon completion of the autopsy. Tox screen came back showing alcohol and a significant quantity of LSD in her system."

"Acid?" Dez said. "We don't see much of that on the streets."

"Not anymore," Flynn said. "But it's available to those who want it." He clicked into another area of the report, opening a series of autopsy photos. Gabriella had a scattering of tattoos, including what appeared through partial decomposition to be a trifecta on the back of her neck and a pentagram on her ankle. It was the one on her right forearm that had Dez sitting further forward.

"There it is," Dez said. "The black candle." His eyes went to Sully, who had yet to utter a word. "What are you thinking, Sull?"

Sully glanced from Dez to Flynn. "Does that file give an exact location where she was found?"

Dez knew the reason for the question without having to ask. "God, this is going to be another ghost hunt, isn't it?"

12

THE KIMOTAN RIVER had swelled to levels Sully had never seen, rushing dangerously close to houses along the shores visible from the North Bank Bridge.

They'd foregone the trip back to the Black Fox. Sully fully expected to find water in the basement, but he'd just have to hope for the best and deal with it later. Right now, there was something more important to do.

Their route took them over the river and east along Edgewater Road where it followed the North Kimotan that side of The Forks. A half-hour drive along the rain-soaked thoroughfare took them past the city proper and to the long stretch of rapids after which KR was named. If they kept driving, they'd end up at McCoy Falls and the town halfway down to its base that shared its name. The town was a picture postcard of old-world charm and dignified beauty, a place of seasonal festivals, lazy Sunday drives and families picnicking in the park.

Sully hated the place.

It had been his last stop on the foster home circuit before he'd been placed with the Braddocks. Flynn had taken pity on him after the KRPD—contracted to provide service to McCoy Falls—responded to a fatal house fire at Sully's then-residence. Only seven-year-old Sully and a second foster child managed to escape the blaze. Both boys were questioned with brutal enthusiasm by certain members of the KRPD until Flynn put a stop to it.

The investigation quickly cleared both boys when witnesses reported seeing a girl run from the scene.

Sully had seen the ghost of his foster father in the moments after he and the other boy left the house. But Mr. Blake hadn't seen him, and Sully hoped to keep it that way. He knew the bad-tempered and abusive man was still down there somewhere, and that he'd latch onto Sully the moment he sensed him.

Sully shook the memory off, the need to return to his current predicament ridding him of the previous one.

According to the file Flynn had pulled up, Gabriella's body had made it partway through the rapids before a current took her to the sheltered side of the large rock where joggers had eventually made the grisly find.

There would be no joggers today, no one insane enough to be exploring the area in this weather save Sully and, by extension, Dez. For his part, Dez looked to be working up the courage he'd need to step out of the safety of the SUV, having parked in the lot that marked the beginning of one of the area's walking trails.

Sully smiled sympathetically as his brother blew out a tension-filled breath. "You don't have to come."

"The river's raging, Sull."

Enough said. Dez couldn't see his kid brother Aiden, but he was haunted by him nonetheless. It didn't escape Sully that Aiden, then just five, had been found along a riverbank. Fifteen years was a long time, and nowhere near long enough.

And so Sully and Dez left the vehicle together and started down the path. Flynn had outfitted them with plastic ponchos and firm warnings about getting too close to the water, and Sully felt the benefit of both as they sighted the river coming into view through the trees.

The water roared as it coursed through rock and forest, cresting large boulders ordinarily out of reach. Already parts of the path were underwater, and Dez and Sully had to make their own route through the trees to the north, holding onto trunks, roots and large rocks for purchase as the muddy slopes threatened to wash them toward the rapids.

Dez's voice sounded from behind Sully. "This isn't a good idea."

Sully was inclined to agree, but saying it out loud wouldn't make the situation any better. Good idea or not, they didn't have an option. *He* didn't have an option. Not if they were going to find Sparrow.

"How much further?" Sully asked instead.

"It can't be far. It seemed to me it would only be about a five-minute walk from the parking lot. Even accounting for us moving slower, we've got to be close."

Though he had yet to see anything, Sully sensed the spot ahead pulling on his gut, causing a familiar roiling inside him. He didn't say as much to Dez; the poor guy was having enough trouble as it was. But she was here. Sully could feel her presence growing stronger as they returned to the muddy path, perceiving he would see Gabriella if he searched the area around a large rock outcropping up ahead.

Dez ran into his back as Sully stopped, having reached the section of path that would allow him a view down to the spot, now directly south of them.

Dez didn't ask, remaining quiet, but his actions said plenty as he edged in closer to Sully. He maintained his silence for a good minute before dread and curiosity got the better of him. "Do you see her?"

Sully shook his head, his gaze remaining fixed on the relatively calm waters on the sheltered side of the rock. "Not yet."

"But she's here?"

Sully nodded and Dez, heaving a breath, fell back into silence and closed the remaining couple of inches that separated the brothers so that Sully could feel Dez's solid arm against his own. It wasn't clear who was supporting whom, but it didn't really matter as Sully at last spotted a hint of movement from the water. A dark form took shape beneath the rapids, growing as it drifted toward shore. Toward them.

Within moments, Sully could make out the shape of a woman. And then a face—beautiful even in death—broke the surface.

Gabriella moved unhindered through the water, clad in a dark T-shirt that hung, sodden, from her slight shoulders and small breasts. She took one last step before standing just this side of the large rock outcropping, dark, shining eyes fixed on him.

Sully guessed Gabriella—visible only from ribcage up—was standing near where the shore was supposed to be, and so at the spot where her body had been found. And he knew without hearing the words what she was asking of him.

"She wants me to go down to her."

Sully took a step forward only to be stopped by Dez's hand grasping the back collar of his jacket, shirt and poncho, wet knuckles ice cold against Sully's upper spine.

"You're not going down there, Sull. No way in hell. Look at it."

"I don't think I have a choice."

"Damn right you don't have a choice. I'm not letting you go down there."

Dez's hand still firmly knotted into his clothing, Sully opted to speak to Gabriella. "Can you come up here? I can't get all the way to you. It's too dangerous."

She didn't move, answering his question without forming words he'd never hear.

"Dez, I have to go down."

"Damn it." In Sully's peripheral vision, Dez scrubbed a hand along his face. "Okay. Okay, but we go down there together. You stay within grabbing distance, you got that?"

That suited Sully fine, and Dez released him to provide them both with two free hands to hold onto the trees that supported their descent down the slope. Dez materialized beside Sully as he closed to within ten feet of the rushing water.

"Close enough, Sully," he said.

But Gabriella didn't seem to share that view, remaining where she was. She was more visible to him here, enabling Sully to see the bruises wrongly put down to accident or misadventure. Unless he closed the gap, Sully knew that was all he'd see.

And he needed more.

"She's not moving," he said.

"Where is she?"

Sully extended an arm, pushing the poncho away enough that he could point out the spot. "There. Near the far edge of that rock."

"Sully, no. That's something like fifteen feet in. You're not going in there. The current's too strong."

"Dez—"

"I said no. Find another way."

"Look, there won't be a strong current if I hug the rock. If I keep right up against it, I can reach her."

Dez didn't appear even remotely close to convinced. "Look, I think I've still got the camping supplies in the hatch, and I always keep some rope there. Let's go get it. I can tie you to me and use one of the trees to set up a pulley."

There was no sense arguing. Except in one respect. "You go. I'll wait here."

"Screw that, man."

"I won't go in until you get back, okay? I promise. I just don't want to lose sight of her."

"I'm not sure your promises cut much with me anymore."

"I know I screwed up today, Dez. I won't do it again. Anyway, I know what you went through as a kid. I'm not going to put you through that again, all right? I mean it. I'll wait here."

Dez studied Sully's eyes for a few seconds, and Sully knew he'd passed the test when Dez turned and started to clamber back up the slope.

But not without a parting warning. "You move one inch, man, I swear I'll tie you to the roof of the car for the ride back to town."

Sully watched Dez until he could see he'd made it back up to the path. But when he returned his attention to the water, Gabriella was gone.

"Oh, hell." Dez's name was on Sully's lips as he started to turn to tell him he'd lost the ghost. But before a sound had passed his lips, he heard his brother shout.

Not a word, but a startled yell.

Through eyes widened in fear and desperation, Sully looked for his brother. But it wasn't on the path he found him.

Dez was sliding down the slope. Towards the river.

Into the river.

Sully sprinted forward, screaming Dez's name as he searched the violent white waves for any sign of wet copper hair. He spotted his target a second before the water slammed Dez against the side of the rock outcropping.

Unlike the more sheltered side of the rock where Gabriella had emerged, there were no still waters here. It was all pounding white waves and viciously cast-off spray.

And that's where Dez disappeared.

13

HE SCREAMED Dez's name one last time.

There was no point trying again. His brother wouldn't hear him, not with all that water holding him down.

There was no time to call 9-1-1, no way anyone could get here to help. He was all Dez had.

Ripping off the poncho, Sully tossed his still-bagged cellphone onto the ground. He'd need it to call for help as soon as he had his brother out of there.

And he would get him out. There was no other option.

Sully ran into the water, feeling the current catch immediately and sweep his feet out from under him. He hit the water hard, side impacting painfully on a rock beneath him as he was taken fully under. He pushed his hands frantically through the waves, searching blindly for Dez as he fought his own panic over the inability to breathe.

He could feel nothing but rock and rushing water.

The sickening thought came uninvited. Maybe Dez wasn't even here, already swept away into the rapids.

Toward the falls.

The panic gave Sully an injection of adrenaline as he continued the search. Seconds passed, feeling like endless hours before

Sully's hand collided not with rock or broken tree branch, but with a limb. A very human limb. Sully wrapped hands around what he recognized as Dez's solid bicep and pulled. Toward what, he had no idea. He just knew anywhere was better than here, pinned to the bottom under the weight of crashing water.

He fought to get his legs under him as he reestablished his hold on Dez, moving to wrap arms around his brother's barrel of a chest. But as hard as he tried, he couldn't find any purchase on the slippery river bottom, particularly not with the current continuing to beat down.

Consciousness was on its way out as Sully's heart sought escape in a steadily harsh drumbeat against his ribcage.

He'd been close to death before, and so recognized the inexplicable calm that stole over him, creating a disturbed clarity in his mind.

Into that Gabriella pressed, her face appearing in front of his as she—like Breanna before her—wrapped firm fingers around Sully's throat.

This time, the effect was negligible, no air to lose and none to be gained. It didn't matter. The connection was made, the image blasting into Sully's brain like a bolt of lightning. There was pain—his own rather than hers, he expected—but it didn't interfere with what he saw through her eyes.

She was dancing on a night-quiet bridge, spinning like a whirling dervish.

She looked to her outstretched arms as her movement inexplicably pushed bold, black feathers from her pores. It wasn't normal, and yet it seemed the most natural thing to her in that moment.

As she spun, Sully—through her eyes—saw the blurry image of a man standing near her, yet far enough back he wouldn't be struck as she giddily continued to whip her body around. Sully knew there were words being spoken but, as usual, he couldn't hear them, locked into only what he could see.

As if it were his own, Sully felt the dizziness and the nausea that followed as she finally stopped, her movement hurling her against the guardrail of the bridge. Leaning over it, her eyes drifted downwards. Her vision was still spinning, still caught up in that dance, and it remained that way as she tried to look at the man as he drew closer.

The man—nothing but a rushed blur as her eyes continued to spin—was saying something to her. And while Sully couldn't hear her words, he could sense the turn of her thoughts: "Maybe he's right. Maybe I can fly."

Sully felt rather than heard her laugh, a wild rumble that echoed within her consciousness as she climbed over the railing, holding to it with long, black-taloned fingers as her feathers rustled in the breeze. She began to let go, to release the railing as she gazed at the slowly stilling river of stars far, far below.

And she knew she had to look, to make sure she was prepared for this maiden flight.

The feathers were gone. Talons mere fingernails, painted black to match her shirt. His hand was on hers, his candle tattoo that matched her own visible in the roll of his sleeves. She knew he would pull her away from here, help her back to the safety that waited on the other side of that railing.

Instead, she felt fingers wrap around her throat, squeezing, digging in just enough to tell her he was not simply having fun with her. It wasn't enough to cut off her air or her cry of terror, possibly not even to bruise.

But it was enough to let her know his intentions.

He was going was to kill her.

Illogical survival instinct had her releasing the railing with her dominant right hand so she could try to pull his hands away, the need to free herself from his grasp outweighing every other risk. His fingers felt large next to hers, large and firm and unyielding, enough to necessitate the use of her other hand to try to pry them free. And, while she had yet to make any real purchase in a phys-ical sense, her actions had their desired outcome as, in one fluid movement, he released her throat.

Now there was only her and the river below, and a railing she couldn't find with fumbling fingers.

She fell.

The roar of air rushing past was all she knew.

That and the dark water of the Kimotan speeding toward her.

Sully didn't feel her impact; rather, he felt one of his own.

There was a solid thump against his front, one that didn't come from Dez—still held tight in his arms—but rather through him. A second one came, then a third, the impact behind each growing steadily stronger.

And then, by some miracle, Sully felt his head break the surface, his body and Dez's pushed free of the current. Sully took in what he could of a gasped breath before his lungs rebelled, choking out the water he'd swallowed. Opening his eyes, he saw they were just a few feet from shore. Gabriella stood a short distance away, where they'd just been, and Sully nodded his thanks before it occurred to him she might well have been responsible for their ending up in here in the first place.

With Dez's head cradled between jaw and shoulder, Sully struggled with the larger man's dead weight, working to get them back to shore.

Dread formed over those words in his brain—dead weight—lending Sully added strength to finish pulling his older brother free of the water.

Dez wasn't breathing. That part was obvious immediately. Sully grunted as he turned Dez onto his side, delivering a series of sharp blows to his back which expelled the water and blessedly started Dez coughing and vomiting up river water and whatever he'd had for lunch all over Sully's knees.

Sully had never been so happy to be puked on. Alternating between coughing and uttering reassuring words to Dez, Sully folded himself over his big brother in as much of a hug as their position would allow. His relief heightened when Dez's right arm wrapped around his legs in response.

Dez managed to get out a handful of choked words between the coughing spasms. "Never again, Sully. Never again."

———————

For at least the third time that day, Sully was about to catch hell from someone he loved. This time, it was Eva.

The latest chastisement came as the two of them were waiting on tests that would reveal if a blow Dez had taken to the head was anything serious.

"Damn it, Sully. I warned you, didn't I? Why would you do this, huh?"

Sully had already been checked out and had escaped with bruises, bumps and scrapes. And one hell of a case of guilt. He'd spoken to his brother on the way back into town, had learned Dez felt hands shove him from the path. Hands they both knew weren't attached to a living, breathing person. Sully tried repeatedly to apologize to his brother, but Dez—the consummate big brother—wouldn't allow it.

Now all Sully could do was make the same attempt with Eva.

"I know. You're right. It's my fault he was there, that he got hurt. I knew he wasn't crazy about the idea. I didn't think I had a choice."

"You had a choice," she said. "You just chose your ghosts over your brother. Think about it. Every time you go off and do something stupid, he follows. He could have died today. He almost did. Is that what you want?"

Sully had been staring at his knees, but the question had him snapping eyes on her. "Of course it isn't. How can you even ask me something like that?"

"Because in a way, it's fine for you. If he dies, you still get to see him. I don't."

Ordinarily, those words would have had Eva staring at his disappearing back. But they had sparked tears in her, and Sully knew he couldn't walk away from her if she was crying. Especially her. Between Dez and Eva, Dez was the one far more likely to shed tears—over upsetting news, a stressful day at work or a sappy movie. Eva just wasn't a crier.

"Eva—"

"Just leave me alone, all right? I need a few minutes by myself."

Sully obeyed—to a point. They were in one of the ER's soft rooms and he had no intention of going anywhere. He needed to know Dez was okay, and he wasn't leaving Eva until then. So he left the room but took one of the chairs immediately outside the door, trying to decide how long to give her before going back in to check on her. He knew Eva well, knew her words had been sparked more by fear for Dez than anger at Sully. What she said had hurt, but not so much for the way it had been said as for the fact he knew it was true.

He hadn't called Flynn or Mara yet, didn't want to worry them until they had some news. Anyway, Kayleigh was with Mara, and Sully knew Dez wouldn't want his daughter seeing him until he could stand on his own two feet to greet her with a grin and a big hug.

Sully lowered his face into his hands, combing through his still-drying hair as he breathed out a pained sigh and closed his eyes. The moment he did, all he could see was Gabriella's face in front of his in the water, her ghostly yet unsettlingly solid fingers coming to wrap around his throat. The image of her dancing, buoyed by drug-induced euphoria, whirling in her own breeze.

Falling ....

Sully's eyes popped open. But he didn't just see his own boot tops. A second pair of feet stood just in front of his.

Sully's shock came in a strangled cry as he took in the ghost of Breanna Bird. Her hands were reaching out to him, so close her fingers nearly brushed his nose.

"Not now, okay?" he whispered. "Not here."

Not ever, if he had any say in the matter. Dez and Eva had

been right. The danger was growing. And now it was affecting Dez.

As far as Sully was concerned, that crossed an unforgivable line.

But Breanna wasn't leaving; her hands remained clenched together. They were moving now, as if crushing something between them.

"I said I can't." He risked raising his voice a little. "Don't you get it? I can't do this anymore. Please leave me alone. Please, just leave me alone."

Breanna's hands parted and Sully watched as purple petals—iris petals—fluttered to the ground, settling around his feet.

The message was clear enough.

Sully exhaled a resigned sigh. "Sparrow's going to die, isn't she?"

Breanna's head gave an almost imperceptible nod.

"Soon?"

Another nod. Damn it.

"Can you lead me to her?"

This time, a head-shake, no.

Sully knew he'd never survive it if anything happened to Dez because of him. And he could try, and try hard, to ignore the dead. But he couldn't turn his back on the living. And, for now at least, that included Sparrow.

"I'll help you, all right? I just need to deal with some stuff here. I won't be long."

Eva's voice, sounding from over his shoulder, made Sully jump. "You're talking to one of them, aren't you?"

Sully hadn't had a chance to answer before Eva turned toward what, to her, would just be empty air. "You leave my family alone, you hear me? They're mine, not yours. Your problems aren't ours, and it's not up to us to fix them."

"Eva, you realize you're a police officer, right?"

"Shut up. Is she the one who pushed Dez?"

"No. It wasn't her."

Eva's eyes widened. "God, how many are there?" Again, she didn't wait on a reply before returning attention to the ghost. "If you hurt anyone I love, I swear to God I'll have you exorcised."

"Eva?"

"What?"

"She's gone. And, just so you know? You can't exorcise ghosts. That's demons."

"Feels like the same thing to me." Eva's expression lost its fury. "You said she's gone but it's not for good, is it?"

Sully forced what he could of a smile. There was no point answering. She wouldn't want to hear what he had to tell her.

"Can we talk for a minute? In the room?"

Sully followed Eva and took the seat on the couch she was patting beside her. She met his eye, but only for a moment, shifting to stare at the wall across the room. The moment of eye contact was long enough that he could see something inside her had broken.

"I'm sorry," she said. "I shouldn't have said the things I said to you a few minutes ago. You know I love you, right?"

She wouldn't see him nod, so he answered in words. "Yeah."

"And I know you care about us as much as we do you."

"You guys are everything to me."

For some reason, that drew a noise from Eva's throat that sounded suspiciously like a choked sob. But Eva didn't break, sucking back her emotion and concealing the pain beneath a mask of stone. "I don't want to say this to you, but I need you to give us some space. Dez adores you, but he has a daughter to worry about. I know you can't help the things you see, and I know you feel like you have a duty to them, the same way Dez and I have a duty to protect the public while we're on the job. But you need to do something for me, for Dez, even for yourself. If you're in the middle of something like this, then I don't want you coming around or asking for his help. If anything happened to him, it would destroy all of us. Me, Kayleigh, your parents, you. All of us. He's our heart, Sully, and if he stops beating, we're all lost. Do you understand?"

Sully was working past the lump in his own throat, but hadn't quite gotten there when he choked out the words she needed to hear. "I understand."

The doctor chose that moment to come in, and it was just as well they were in a hospital waiting on word about a loved one as that would provide adequate explanation for the tears in both their eyes.

There was good news, at least. No sign of a head injury and no indication of any damage from Dez's having gone briefly without air. The doctor—one it appeared Dez and Eva knew, likely through work—wanted him here for another few hours to monitor him, and advised Dez book off sick for the night shift he was supposed to be starting soon. But all in all, it seemed Dez had avoided major repercussions from his near-drowning.

The doctor left after providing the location of Dez's room in the ER.

And, for Sully, there was only one thing left to say. "Tell Dez I love him, okay, Eva? And tell him I'm sorry."

The iris petals were still on the floor outside the soft room door as Sully walked down the hall.

Out the sliding glass doors.

Out into the storm.

14

THERE WAS no point beating around the bush. If Marc Echoles was the man responsible for the deaths of Breanna Bird and Gabriella Aguado, then that was where Sully was going.

The problem was, he didn't know where to go.

It was closing in on seven in the evening, and the doors to the university's arts building were locked tight. He pulled out his phone, doing a quick 4-1-1 search of the name, but discovered Marc was unlisted. Naturally. Anyone who was a practicing Wiccan was likely to want to remain unlisted in order to avoid the freaks—both occultists and Christian zealots—who might come banging down his door.

Ordinarily, this was the point at which Sully might ask Dez, Eva or Flynn to check Marc's address, an easy enough task since it had been the location of a break-in a year ago. Now that was no longer an option.

But that gave him a thought. It had been a college kid the police had picked up for the incident, so it was likely at least a few students knew where Marc lived.

The next problem would be figuring out where to find them.

Sully had learned earlier that Marc was the professor of two sociology classes: social deviance and history of the occult. Sully could start by picking his way through gatherings of students in dorm common areas or the university's bar. Or he could take what he hoped would be the quicker approach.

While most of the buildings were closed, the library wasn't one of them. As he sloshed through the lobby to a set of elevators, he added his own wet footprints to numerous others. Final papers were more or less in now, and it was time for students to start cramming for summer session exams.

A board next to the elevator told him what he needed to know, and he made his way up to the fourth floor where the sociology and psychology sections were. From there, it was just a matter of picking his way through the stacks until he found the right area.

He located it near the back of the library, a couple rows in. There was no one currently in the stacks here, where books on the occult and new age were kept, but there were a handful of students sitting at the tables. From a gap between books and upper shelf, Sully scanned the students, trying to catch a glimpse of book titles. Unfortunately, most of the books were open, so that was out of the question.

The solution came in the form of a pentagram, a small silver pendant that dangled from a black velvet choker around the neck of a girl with long, glossy black hair and ear buds dangling down the front of her black shirt. Turning back to the shelf, Sully scanned them for something he could use as an icebreaker. He took his time, working hard to summon up the courage to head over there and speak with her. He'd never been good at approaching people he didn't know, let alone pretty girls, and it felt even worse given he was going in with a lie.

He knew how to lie; there had been times in his life he'd had to. He hated doing it, but there was no getting around it. Not tonight.

He located and pulled out a book about the Salem witch trials and circled the stacks, approaching the girl with the choker. He could make out the sound of a Rob Zombie song coming from the earphones, but she still glanced up at his approach.

"Mind if I sit here?" he asked in his library voice, indicating the chair opposite her.

The girl grinned and shook her head a little too fast. Sully had never been much of a judge of these things, always felt he was either too thin when next to Dez, that his hair was too shaggy, or that he wasn't outgoing enough to last in the dating scene. And yet, he never seemed to have trouble finding girls who looked at him the way this one was right now, smile lingering around her lips as she pulled the earbuds from her ears.

It seemed Rob Zombie was taking an intermission.

He was still trying to figure out how to start the conversation in a way that wouldn't immediately give away his purpose when she settled the problem for him.

"Salem witch trials, huh?"

"Yeah. I saw a show on it and was thinking about taking a class in that area. I'm just fumbling around right now with a bunch of classes that don't mean anything to me."

"Well, as it happens, you've just sat next to an expert. I can—"

She was interrupted by a sharp shushing from an annoyed young woman at the next table.

Sully's tablemate rolled her eyes and leaned over to whisper to him. "Tell you what. Leave the book and come with me. I'll buy you a coffee and tell you anything you ever wanted to know about witches."

"Aren't you studying?"

"If I read another line, I'm going to start looking for a window to jump out of. I need a distraction, and you're a good one. Come on."

There was no time for talk on the way to the campus coffee house—open and doing decent business thanks to the cramming students—as the wind and rain now held so much force they were forced to sprint.

They ordered coffee, Sully getting the strongest he could find given his expectation he could easily be up all night on this search. A table at the back came open just as they got their order, and Sully's companion made a beeline for it, achieving a narrow win over a cranky-looking young guy who'd just come in from outside.

"So what's your name?" she asked, taking a measured sip of her coffee.

"Sullivan. What's yours?"

"Takara, but I prefer to go by Ara. My parents ...." She didn't elaborate, as if that statement said it all.

"So, not to assume or anything, but are you a practicing witch?"

"I dabble, I guess. I'm not part of a coven or anything. But I read a lot, and I've tried out a few spells." She broke into a coy smile. "I'm hoping maybe one of them actually worked."

It dawned on Sully what she meant, and he made a show of focusing on his coffee. Where Dez panicked when forced to talk about the occult or supernatural, Sully dreaded conversations like this. Not that he wasn't interested; Ara was incredibly beautiful. But there was something unnatural to him in that type of chat, a pretence he'd never been able to master.

"You're shy," she said, picking up on the crush of signals he knew he was emitting without trying. "That's cute."

He managed a smile—and that would be about all he'd manage unless he could successfully steer this conversation back to his intended topic.

"You said you know about witchcraft," he said.

She laughed, and he found he liked the sound. "Okay, okay, point taken. What do you want to know? Ask me anything."

He'd given it some thought prior to approaching her at the library, and decided he'd have to play it through a bit. He asked a couple questions and let her ramble a bit about pagan religious history, the birth of Wicca and the historical persecution of women and social misfits. He didn't have to feign interest, but he did find he struggled to hang onto her words. The longer he sat here, the more he was drawn in by her deep brown, almond-shaped eyes, how they sparkled when she laughed ....

"You still with me, Sullivan?"

"Uh, yeah, sorry. Just didn't sleep much last night. Listen, I was doing some checking into classes and I noticed Marc Echoles teaches some stuff in this area. Are you familiar with him?"

"Oh, yeah. Everyone knows Marc. He's your man if you want to learn about anything pagan or occult. And he practices the craft too, so there's that."

"Didn't I hear someone broke into his house last year?"

"Yeah, some nut job, probably looking for something to pawn for drug money."

"Does he live near here?" Sully was grasping, he knew. No way this was a natural topic of conversation. But Ara's suspicions didn't seem to have been triggered.

"Yeah, actually. There are a few professors who bought up places around here. Marc's is on Brightmore Crescent, only about three blocks away. Kind of a fitting place for a practicing witch, given that it kind of looks like a miniature castle. It's got a turret and everything. Naturally, the turret is where he keeps his altar. Not that I've seen it firsthand or anything, but that's what people say."

She leaned closer, grinning as if about to impart a delicate conspiracy. "Some people even say he performs human sacrifices. Houses around here have old stone cellars and solid foundations. People could scream for hours in the basement, and no one would ever hear them."

Sully guessed he looked how he felt as Ara broke into a wild giggle. "You should see your face. It's just a story, Sullivan. No one actually believes it, you know."

And that, right there, could be just the problem. If it were true, and no one believed it, who could say how much Marc Echoles had gotten away with already?

PRYING himself away from Ara only after accepting her phone

number, Sully headed back out into the rain and hoofed it over to Brightmore Crescent.

He was thoroughly soaked through within minutes, a state that was fast becoming second nature. The storm would have to let up eventually, and Sully couldn't wait for the moment when his clothing didn't feel like it weighed more than he did.

Ara hadn't provided an address, and Sully didn't dare ask for one. It was welcome surprise enough that he'd made it as far as he had, finding someone who knew how to find the professor.

And Ara's directions and description proved more than enough. Sully forced himself to walk rather than run through Brightmore Crescent, not wanting to stick out more than he already did. No one would willingly be out in this right now, at least no one with all their mental faculties intact. The last thing he needed was to have the police show up and start questioning him as a suspicious person.

Although, if he were honest, the idea of having some armed backup nearby didn't feel like such a bad thing right now.

The turreted house was easy to find on the small crescent as the architecture appeared unique to this property. Sully could make out a couple lights on inside, one somewhere toward the back of the house on the main floor, visible through what he imagined was a living room window; the other up in the turret itself.

Sully didn't stand there long, ducking through an open wrought-iron gate framed by a pair of elm trees. Leaning against one of the thick trunks, he sought to conceal himself in the shadow created by a nearby streetlight. He needed a moment to get his head screwed on before he attempted an approach. If he was going in there, he needed to be ready for anything.

Naturally, the power chose that moment to go out, lights disappearing from the windows, streetlights extinguishing in one fluid blink. It should have been a relief for someone hiding in shadow, waiting for the solidification of courage that might not ever happen to any satisfying extent. And yet Sully was unnerved by the distinct feeling he was being watched. Being *seen*.

The proof came not a minute later.

"Come inside, Sullivan. You'll catch your death out there."

Sully froze, fingers gripping at the bark of the tree behind him as his breath caught. He knew it was pointless, and yet here he was, stalled out next to the tree when it was plenty clear he wasn't fooling anyone.

"Sullivan? I know you're by the tree. I can see you. Come inside."

And so he moved. One foot in front of the other as he did as told. This was why he'd come here, to find a way inside the house of the tattooed man. Only now, he wasn't so sure. No one knew he was here.

Marc Echoles stood on the other side of the door, waiting patiently in the entryway with one of those solid-looking flashlights. One that had a long, heavy, stainless steel grip that could brain a guy in three blows. Sully crossed the threshold, stepping into the pool of light Marc created for him on the floor.

"You're in luck," Marc said. "I'd just boiled some water for tea when the power finally gave up the battle. It's been flickering for the past hour, trying to make up its mind. Take off your boots and your jacket. I'll show you to the main floor bathroom and get you something dry to put on. Then you can tell me what brings you here."

It wasn't until Sully was in the half-bath, peeling off his wet layers, that it occurred to him he hadn't yet uttered a word to Marc.

The professor had given him a pair of drawstring fleece pyjama bottoms, an oversized hooded sweatshirt and a pair of thick wool socks. Sully waited a couple minutes, standing there naked as he both allowed his skin to dry and tried to think through what he would do should this situation take a turn for the worse. He took the opportunity to check his phone, finding one missed call from Eva but nothing more, suggesting Dez was still in the ER and had yet to discover Sully had left. Of course, it could also mean Dez had rethought the situation and decided he was pissed at his brother after all for almost getting him killed, but that was a possibility Sully didn't think he could face right now. He'd have plenty of apologizing to do later, regardless, and it would be easier if Dez was willing to sit and hear him out.

Eva had left a voicemail, and Sully reluctantly listened in case it contained an update about his older brother. "Sully, I need you to give me a call. Dez is fine, but I'm not. I was talking out of my ass earlier and I'm sorry. Please, just call me, okay?"

Sully held the phone in his hand, debating whether he should call just to let someone know where he was. After a minute weighing the options, he clicked the phone off and dropped it back into its temporary plastic bag case. Eva had become like a big sister to him, and he knew she and Dez would be over here within minutes—with or without the requisite hospital release—if he filled her in. He'd already almost lost Dez once today; he'd be damned if he let that happen again, to Dez or to Eva. No fear he was currently battling was a bigger beast than that one, the idea of someone he loved being put in danger on his behalf.

Using the glow of the small flashlight Marc had provided, he put on the dry clothes and prepared to step out of the bathroom. He paused with his hand on the doorknob, then reached back and snagged his phone from the counter, dropping it into the sweat-shirt's right pocket. Even if he called no one, the idea that he could made him feel a little better. He then rifled through his discarded jeans until his hand settled over his foldable pock-etknife, and he slipped that, too, inside the pocket—a second, equally welcome reassurance.

Taking a quick, deep breath, he turned the handle, preparing himself to face whatever was waiting for him.

15

Eva was upset about something.

But it wasn't until they hit the hallway that would take them out of the ER that Dez realized it was about more than the fact his idiocy had nearly gotten him killed.

It was the iris petals that did it, had him drawing up short and forcing Eva to a halt next to him.

Dez pointed to the chair beneath which the purple petals rested. "Was Sully sitting there?"

"Listen, about that—"

"Was he sitting there?"

"Yeah, he was. How did you know that?"

"Shit. Where is he?"

"Dez, we need to talk for a minute."

"Where's Sully, Eva?"

"I don't know, okay? I've tried calling, but he isn't picking up."

Dez let that sink in, didn't like where it took him. "God-dammit, Sully. Hon, I need your phone."

Dez's own phone had bit the biscuit in the water, giving him one more thing he needed to take care of tomorrow. But right now, he had bigger fish to fry, and he pounded Sully's name in Eva's contacts as he made the call. He listened to the phone ring through to voicemail before trying it again. And again. He hated texting, his large fingers useless on the keypad, but he fumbled through a quick one anyway, demanding a return message. On the fourth attempt at a phone call, his blood pressure having risen significantly with worry, he left a voicemail.

"Sully, I'm with Eva. I need you to call me, right now. And I swear to you, man, if you're doing anything stupid, I'm going to pound your scrawny ass."

Eva nodded as she took her phone back. "I'm sure that'll do it. Who wouldn't respond to that kind of message of love and concern?"

"He is doing something stupid, isn't he?"

"I don't know, Dez. I really don't. Maybe he just went back to the Black Fox to make sure it hasn't floated away."

Dez shook his head. "No, not with those petals sitting there." He led Eva back into a soft room, closing the door and relaying the explanation where it wasn't likely to be heard by anyone who would think he should be committed as a result. Eva already had part of the story, but it took a few minutes to provide the rest—by the end of which Sully still hadn't called back.

"Dez, sweetie, I need to tell you something."

Dez's focus was on the phone, fingers picking out Sully's number in the recent call list. "In a sec."

"Dez—"

"Right away. I just need to get ahold of my dumb brother." But the phone rang through again to voicemail. Dez tried three more times before returning the phone to his wife.

"Why isn't he answering?" Dez had asked the question rhetorically, and yet Eva looked like she had an answer she wasn't excited to provide. Her face was flushed, and Dez found himself wondering whether she'd looked this way a moment ago when she'd been trying to get his attention.

"Dez, I need to tell you something. Let's sit down, okay?"

"God, what?"

He allowed her to lead him to a vinyl-covered couch and sat next to her as she bit at her lower lip and launched into what sounded to Dez like a confession. "I need to tell you something."

"You already said that."

"Just let me say it, okay? I was so scared after what happened today that I wasn't thinking. I said some things to Sully I shouldn't have. I blamed him, or at least the things around him, for what happened to you. And I asked him to give you space, to stay away from you, when he's dealing with something like this."

"Why would you say that?" Dez didn't snap the words. How could he when she was sitting there, struggling to meet his eye and swiping at the tears that had escaped down her cheeks? He'd known Eva since police college. They'd fallen in love there, had decided to spend the rest of their lives together at that point. Rarely during the few years they'd known each other had Dez seen Eva cry. The last thing he wanted to do was make it worse, even after what she'd just said.

"I was so scared for you," she said. "You don't see what he sees. You don't see the threat until it's too late. And I know you, Dez. You'd do anything for the people you love, even die for them. I've always known I can't lose you, that the idea of it terrifies me so much that I can't even think about it. Today, I had no choice. I had to face one of my darkest fears. And I don't like what I became."

Dez pulled her gently to him, holding her against his chest. He felt her hand press against the thrum of his heart as if to reassure herself—a move that had the heat building up behind his eyes as his own tears threatened to form and fall.

"I know what it's like to deal with fear, Evie. I was only eight when we lost Aiden, and that made death real to me. I've lived ever since with the knowledge it could happen to anyone I love at any time. And I vowed I would do everything in my power to make sure I don't go through that again. So, yeah, I'd do anything for the people I love. But you can't bench me because of it, okay? This is who I am. You're not saving me if I'm still alive only because I wasn't able to be there to help someone close to me. If someone I love died because I somehow failed them … that isn't something I think I could live with. You need to understand something, babe. I went downhill fast after Aiden, and no one could pull me out of the pit. Not Mom and Dad, not the counsellor they took me to, not my friends. No one. It was Sully who did it. He saved me, Eva. And if I have to, I will spend the rest of my life saving him back."

"I'll help you find him."

"I'll be fine. Head to Mom and Dad's and stay there with Kayleigh. I'll—"

Eva pushed away far enough she could meet his eye. Grief had been replaced by the determination he so much admired and loved about her. "I said I'll help you find him. Don't take that as an offer or a suggestion. It's a promise. To both of you."

And there was no arguing with that.

IF THERE WAS EVER GOING to be an opportunity to search the house for Sparrow, it was now.

The power was still out, bathing the interior in darkness as Sully crept along the hallway outside the bathroom door, flashlight in hand but off for now. Somewhere to the left, he could hear the sound of porcelain against granite and a quiet humming Sully assumed was Marc's. There was little light showing as Sully passed the spot, just a sliver emanating from beneath a closed door.

Sully was banking on it that the basement steps could be found somewhere toward the back of the house, although it occurred to him in his search for doors that houses of this vintage sometimes had old root cellars or even bomb shelters in the backyard. If Sparrow was there, Sully would have to find another way later on.

For now, he was here, feeling along the wall for doorknobs,

finally finding one around a corner. Marc's humming sounded louder again and Sully guessed there was a rear access to the kitchen here, given he was likely in or near a mudroom separating the kitchen from the house's rear exterior door.

Sully had managed to make it this far, avoiding creaky floorboards by hugging the walls. Now he had potentially squeaky hinges to contend with as he slowly turned the knob in his grip and eased the door open an inch or two. So far, so good. Now it was an inch-by-inch job until he could gain enough space to slip through.

He'd made it to about inch three when he realized he couldn't hear anything. Not hinges, not muffled cries for help from a missing girl.

Not Marc's quiet humming.

"Looking for something?"

Sully spun in place to see a light click on, revealing Marc standing a couple feet in front of him. Sully couldn't make out much of Marc's face as the light moved from Sully's chest to the floor, leaving it unclear whether the professor was angry, suspicious or outright homicidal right now.

Sully did what he could to erase suspicion in case Marc was edging toward the latter. "I got a little turned around in the dark."

"That's why I gave you a flashlight." Marc's beam fastened onto Sully's left hand which continued to hold the object in question.

"It turned itself off and I couldn't get it to come back on."

Marc reached down and took it from Sully. One click had a second beam partially illuminating the space. "Hmm, looks all right now." Marc brought the beam of the smaller light up to shine into Sully's face for a moment, causing him to squint and turn his face away—opening himself up to attack should Marc choose it.

But no blow came. "Why don't you come into the kitchen so you can tell me what you're really doing here."

It was more an order than a request, one followed by the

extension of Marc's beam along the floor through what Sully could see was indeed a mudroom to the open door leading into the kitchen. "After you," Marc said, and Sully did as told.

He knew the exterior door was to his right as he passed through the mudroom, but he didn't try to make a break for it. It would no doubt be locked, particularly given Marc's experience with the break-in, and Sully wouldn't have time to play with door locks before the older man was on him. He'd have to bide his time, look for an out.

Now inside the kitchen, Marc ushered Sully toward one of several stools along an island upon which two mugs were waiting. Several candles had been lit in here, providing enough light that Marc was able to switch off the flashlights as the two of them reached the island where Sully took one of the stools.

Marc slid a mug toward him.

Sully stared down into the gently steaming liquid and toyed with the string from the teabag in an attempt to disguise his latest anxiety.

"I didn't drug your tea," Marc said. "I don't swing that way, and I don't take things that don't belong to me."

Sully felt the need to address what he thought could be a veiled accusation. "Neither do I."

Marc hoisted himself onto the stool next to Sully where he began the anticipated interrogation. "What are you doing here?"

"I don't know."

It was a lousy attempt at a lie and Sully knew immediately Marc didn't buy it. But the professor appeared to be a patient man, willing to take a more circuitous route to the truth if need be. "If I hadn't seen you outside, what was the plan? Were you going to try to break in?"

"No. How did you know I was out there anyway?"

"You're forgetting I see auras. Yours is like the beacon of a lighthouse, Sullivan. You trying to conceal yourself from people like me is like trying to hide a mammoth behind a kitten. That's how they find you, you know. The dead. You're an incredibly bright light in a dark place and they're like moths to your flame." Marc leaned over, speaking quietly as if wanting to avoid being overheard. "Is that why you're here? Have you seen Mariel?"

Sully shook his head, no.

"Gabriella then?"

That got Marc a nod.

"Is she okay?"

"She's not at peace," Sully said. He thought through how much to tell Marc now that he'd stumbled upon a pretty good legitimate excuse for being here that didn't involve murder and the possibility of a young woman locked in his cellar. He decided to provide a few truths, see where that took them. Marc wasn't easily led down the primrose path, but then neither was Sully. Perhaps the only blessing to having an early childhood like his was the honed ability to read people. When the means to avoid a beating rested in your spotting and accurately assessing the meaning behind the throb of a vein, the twitch of an eye or the turn of a mouth, you learned quickly.

And so Sully turned and fixed his eyes on Marc as he explained.

"It isn't just that I see the dead. I see only those who died because of something bad someone else did to them. Not just murder, I don't think. Sometimes other stuff. I had a hit and run once, killer turned out to be this random drunk guy who didn't want to lose his licence. But most of them are murders."

"So Gabriella …?"

There was nothing Sully could make out on Marc's face but surprise and concern, no discernible sign of knowing.

"She didn't jump or fall. She was forced over."

Sully watched the shock and distress first overtake and then gradually fade from Marc's features, replaced by something he could only describe as resignation.

"You didn't just come here to tell me about this, did you." It was a statement, not a question, but it nonetheless demanded an answer.

"I thought you'd want to know."

Marc had turned from Sully at the upsetting words, but now he faced him again, searching for truths just as Sully was. "No, Sullivan. You thought I already knew. Didn't you?"

"No. I just—"

"Didn't you?" The unanticipated increase in tone and volume in the otherwise-silent house had Sully jumping in his chair.

There was no answer he could provide save the one that could well send Sully to meet Sparrow. And there was no way Marc would believe anything else, not the way those piercing eyes were searching his now, rooting out answers that Sully had hoped to keep to himself, exposing truth within lies. Very little got past Marc Echoles and Sully feared he wouldn't either.

Marc's hand had wrapped around the handle of his solid steel flashlight and Sully, brain twisting now in the grips of fear, pictured tool becoming weapon. Until he was either dead or close enough to it that Marc no longer saw him as a threat.

"I can't do anything about the things I see, and I don't always understand them," Sully said. "All I know is what's right in front of me. Did you have anything to do with Gabriella's death?"

"Is that what she told you?"

"She didn't tell me anything. For some reason, they can't. She just showed me."

"They can't speak to you?"

"They try sometimes. I can't hear them."

For some reason, that caused a change in Marc's countenance. "That's interesting. Do you ever wonder why it is you can see but can't hear?"

"I asked you about Gabriella."

"No, Sullivan. I didn't kill her. If you must know, I was falling in love with her. All right? She was the first truly good thing in my life since Mariel, and had I known the danger she was in, I would have done everything in my power to help her."

"She showed me a tattooed arm like yours. Identical to yours."

"Ah, so that's why you're here. Well, I hate to burst your

investigative bubble, kid, but as I told you previously, everyone in that coven has that tattoo. And a lot of us put it on our forearms. A few have day jobs that absolutely preclude visible tattoos, so they were the exceptions. I promise you, I don't have a murderous bone in my body, and Gabriella was the last person who would have changed that. Does that answer your question?"

"Was there anyone else in the group who would have had motive to kill her? Anyone else who was in love with her?"

"As I said earlier, I'm not at liberty to reveal the names of coven members. But I will give it some thought. I'm not restricted, in my view, from naming a killer. The gentleman you named when you came to see me with your brother. Did you check into him?"

"Kenton Barwell? The tattoo is different, on the wrong arm."

"Just like Ken, always had to be contrary."

"So most others went for the right arm?"

"That's right. I'll tell you what. You keep digging, and so will I. If either of us comes across a coven member with a motive or opportunity concerning Gabriella, we'll let each other know, all right?"

Sully nodded. He wasn't completely sold on Marc not being the killer, but he was starting to move in that direction.

He hadn't checked his phone in a while and felt safe to turn his attention away from Marc long enough to check the screen. One text and eight missed calls from Eva's phone and one call from a number he didn't immediately recognize.

"Mind if I make a call?" he asked. "My brother's in the ER and I've missed a bunch of calls from his wife. I need to check something hasn't happened."

"Of course. I hope everything's okay."

"Me too." Sully headed to the other side of the kitchen for as much privacy as the space would afford and tapped the call button beside Eva's name in his contacts list. Meanwhile, Marc slid off his own stool, took his flashlight and left the kitchen, closing the door behind himself.

Eva's phone didn't even get to the second ring before someone picked up. A flood of relief washed over Sully as he heard Dez's voice.

"Sully? Where are you?"

"Are you okay, D?"

"I'm fine. Where are you?"

That wasn't a question Sully was about to answer. He wasn't sure whether Marc had anything to do with the murders or not, but the last place he wanted Dez at this point was anywhere near this. No way Sully was allowing a repeat of earlier events, particularly when Dez wasn't at his best.

Anyway, telling Dez he'd willingly gone to the house of a suspected killer was likely to end with a solid ass-kicking later.

Then again, he'd never been able to lie to his brother, so he settled on a response that wasn't likely to do much to ease Dez's obvious worry.

"I can't tell you that."

"Tell me where you are, right now."

"No. You already almost died today because of me. It's not happening again."

He didn't wait for the response, clicking the end-call button just as Dez started up again. As expected, the screen of his muted handset showed a call coming in from Eva's phone, but he just hit the button to ignore it and went to check on the other number that had called.

There was a text and several voicemails, most if not all of which were from his brother. He skipped through all of Dez's without listening, unable to deal with the mounting anxiety he could hear in his brother's voice at the start of each consecutive message. But then he came to a voicemail left by someone else.

"Sullivan? It's Paul Dunsmore. You wanted me to call if I got any information for you. I've got something I think you'll want, but I can't get into it over the phone. Come to my place in The Forks as soon as you can."

Two more messages from Dez followed, and Sully skipped

them both. He realized he'd ignored the timestamp on Paul's voicemail, so checked the time on his recents list, finding the call had come in about half an hour ago.

Judging by the weather outside, getting to The Forks wasn't going to be an easy task right now, so Sully opted to call first. If he could get what he needed without heading all the way over there, all the better.

Paul picked up on the first ring. "Sullivan? Where are you?"

Sully scanned the room, assuring himself Marc was nowhere around before answering, keeping his voice quiet enough to not be overheard. "I'm at Marc Echoles's place."

"What? Jesus Christ, kid, get out of there, right now, you hear me? Echoles is dangerous."

"What are you talking about?"

"He did something really bad, life and death bad. You need to get out now."

"You mean murder?"

"Damn it, not over the phone. Not with him around. He knows stuff. He *sees* stuff, you hear me? You need to get out of there and over to me. And hurry up. It's a mess here and people are starting to pack up and bail."

"Can't you come and meet me?"

"No. I'm busy trying to pack up my own stuff. Just get here and I'll explain. Then I'll give you a ride back into Riverview, all right? Just hurry. If you're not here within the hour, I'm going to have to leave."

"Okay. Okay, I'm on my way."

"Good. And Sullivan? You be careful getting out of Echoles's house, all right? Don't turn your back on him."

Sully's phone battery was reading less than twenty per cent when he ended the call, so he turned it off completely, wanting to save the remaining juice in case he should need it later. Naturally, yet another call was coming in from Eva's number as he powered off his handset.

Sully dropped the phone back into its bag, grabbed his

borrowed flashlight off the island and headed for the kitchen's side door, the one he now knew led to the hallway.

The front door, he recalled, was just down the hall. There was no way he'd manage a full search of the house, no way Marc would allow it. And the last thing he wanted right now was to spend another minute around a potential murderer.

He'd made it most of the way down the hall when he found himself illuminated by light and felt a solid hand close over his arm.

"Going somewhere?"

Sully couldn't see Marc's face past the beam, but the voice was as firm as the grip, suggesting the expression wouldn't be far off.

"I need to go see someone."

"In this weather? I don't think so."

"I don't have a choice."

"No," Marc said. "You don't."

16

THE CITY HAD FINALLY GONE into a blackout, the generator-run buildings providing the only semi-reliable light in the storm-cast darkness. A sheet of lightning lit the sky, punctuated by a crack of thunder so intense Dez caught himself jumping in his seat as he eyed the shadow of the house next to them.

He'd been racking his brain trying to figure out where Sully had gone, and he'd settled on a few possibilities. Bulldog was a strong potential, given his own interest in the investigation and the fact he was also proving unreachable by phone. A strong second was Marc Echoles, a man who bore a tattoo matching those Sully's ghosts had shown him.

There were no certainties, but Dez thought there was a strong likelihood Sully had come here—to Marc's university-area home —looking for answers.

"You really think a university professor is behind the murders?" Eva asked. "Seems far-fetched to me. What kind of motive would he have?"

"I'm not worried about motive," Dez said. "All I'm worried about right now is my idiot brother. Wait here."

Even without looking at her, he knew she had to be shaking

her head at him in disbelief. "Right. Screw you, Snowman. Let's go."

There was no sense arguing with a woman who, cool and collected as she typically was, cornered the market on stubborn, so they headed up to the house together, flashlights at the ready. Eva made a motion as if to circle around back, which is how they would have handled this were it a call they were responding to as police officers. But right now all Dez wanted was to find his brother and keep Eva in his sights at the same time, so he snagged her free hand and held on as he thumped the edge of his fist against the door.

They didn't have long to wait before Marc Echoles answered the door.

"What the hell happened to you?" Dez asked, eyes moving to the bag of frozen peas the professor was pressing to his jaw.

"Your brother," he said. "And if you think this is something, you should see the bruise that's forming on my shin."

"So Sully was here?"

" 'Was' being the operative term. I tried to hold him back. I mean, it's Biblical out there. But he wasn't having it."

Dez wasn't sure whether to be amused, damn proud or to simply continue with his current pattern of worry. The third seemed the most likely to win out, so he settled on that.

"Mind if we take a look around?"

Marc's dry chuckle was free of humour. "Let me guess. You think I'm up to something, too, do you?"

"I don't think anything except that my brother's missing and chasing after something I don't really want him to find unless he's got someone at his back. Just let us look around, and we'll be out of your hair."

Marc stood aside and waved an arm grandly at his home's interior as a sweeping yet plenty sarcastic gesture of welcome. "By all means, good sir. But I can assure you, I don't have Sullivan chained up in my oubliette."

Dez stopped and turned to face Marc. "Your what?"

"Oubliette," Eva said. "It's French, from the word meaning to forget. Refers to a room where people were locked up and left to die."

Dez wasn't placated by the definition. "You have one of those?"

"No," Marc said. "Sarcasm, Desmond. Sarcasm."

Dez and Eva cleared the house together, finding no sign of Sully, save a bundle of wet clothes left behind in the main floor half bath. Nor, for that matter, did they find any clues to suggest Marc had ever kept a prisoner here at all.

Marc was waiting by the front door for them. "Satisfied?"

"His clothes are in the bathroom by the kitchen," Dez said. "Why?"

"He was soaked through and freezing. I gave him something warm and dry to put on. It won't be either anymore."

"What's he wearing now?"

"Fleece pyjama bottoms and a dark blue hooded sweatshirt. The university logo is emblazoned on the back."

"Thanks. And sorry about all this, but we needed to check. Did Sully say anything about where he was headed?"

"He didn't seem in the mood to share," Marc said. "Look, all I know is that he said something about needing to go meet with someone. I got the impression he had spoken to somebody on the phone. I don't know what was said or who it was."

With little else to get from Marc at the moment, Dez and Eva thanked him and headed back out to Dez's SUV. Dez's mood had gone from bad to worse, but it wasn't until he tried to catch Eva's eye that he realized he might not be the one most in need of comforting right now. There was no emotion on her face, but Dez read the gathering hopelessness there. It didn't happen often, not to Eva, and when it did, it scared the hell out of him.

He sought to erase it, landing a hand on her shoulder before dropping it to grasp the fingers of her left hand. "Hey, we'll find him, all right?"

"I'm supposed to be trying to make *you* feel better," she said.

"That's what marriage is all about, right? You and me, picking each other's sorry asses out of the emotional gutter."

That got him the smile he was after, albeit a small one. "You really know how to lift a girl's spirits, you know that?"

"It's a gift. Okay, so let's go through this. Someone called Sully and he went to meet them, and given the fact he didn't bother to wait around here, I'm thinking it was urgent. That means it had to have been about Breanna, Sparrow or Gabriella."

"Okay, but that's if you believe Marc. As of now, he's the only one who knows anything about Sully's present movements. And not ten minutes ago, you suspected Marc might have done something to him. He's admitted Sully left him with those injuries. How do we know it ended there?"

That gave Dez reason to pause. "We searched the place top to bottom. There was no sign of Sully or anyone else. You think he's still here somewhere?"

"Honestly, no. I think I buy what Marc told us. I'm just saying we shouldn't dismiss things too quickly. Keep in mind some houses in this neighbourhood have bomb shelters or old root cellars out back."

"Except Marc was bone dry. If he'd taken Sully out back, he would have been soaked through. And those marks on him were fresh."

"So you think he's telling the truth?" Eva asked.

"About Sully taking off on him? Yeah, I do. I'm not so sure yet we can trust Echoles on why he was trying to hold Sully back, but I think we're safe in assuming the guy's not holding anyone there against their will."

"It's still possible he's got someone in the backyard."

Dez grinned. "I thought you weren't onboard with the whole university professor-as-deranged-killer thing."

"You're a bad influence. Okay, so if Sully took off from here, we're going to have to figure out who he was going to see. It's possible it was something as simple as his bar manager calling to ream him out for not showing up at work tonight. But just in case it wasn't, who were you waiting on information from?"

"I haven't heard from Bulldog in a while and I haven't been able to get through to him," Dez said. "That's weird. He's been pretty involved in this given it's centred on his sister and a girl he's started to identify as a niece."

Eva started to suggest Dez try his friend again, but he was well ahead of her. Unfortunately, Bulldog still wasn't of a mind or in a position to pick up, leaving the phone to ring through to voicemail. Leaving Bulldog with instructions to call back as soon as he checked his messages, Dez ended the call, left another fumbling text, and tried Sully again just in case. Unsurprisingly, he got no answer there either.

"Could be they're together," Eva said.

Dez shrugged. "Maybe. Could explain why Bulldog won't pick up."

"You think Bulldog would listen to Sully over you?"

"I tuned the pair of them in earlier today. Could be Bulldog's not overly excited about the idea of talking to me again just yet."

Eva smirked. "And with you probably being so nice and all? Why wouldn't he be? Look, why don't we start hitting up some of the shelters, see if Bulldog's there or if anyone's seen him? Could be we find Bulldog, we find Sully."

"There was someone else we asked for information," Dez said. "Paul Dunsmore. He was going to work some of his contacts, see if he could find us any info on those tattoos."

"But you've got everything you need on those already, don't you? You know they're connected to the Black Candle coven."

"Yeah, but unfortunately, we don't know who was in the coven. That's the key to figuring out who might be behind this and why. Maybe Paul's heard something."

Dez pulled his phone back out and dialed Paul Dunsmore's number, but the call rang through to voicemail and Dez found himself leaving yet another message.

"No one wants to talk to me tonight," Dez said. "Either towers are out of commission, or I've become a social pariah."

"I'm thinking we're going to have to start driving around looking," Eva said. "Where to first? The Black Fox, Bulldog or Dunsmore?"

"We're not far from Riverview. Let's check the Fox and a couple of Bulldog's haunts and then head across the Forks Bridge from there."

"Sounds like a plan. But could we stop by headquarters first? My shift's officially over, and I'm thinking I shouldn't be running around off duty in my police uniform."

"I don't know," Dez said. "The way this night's going, I don't mind the idea of having a sidearm on hand."

It was no surprise, but Dez felt his heart sinking anyway when they arrived at the Black Fox and found no sign of Sully.

Betty Schuster wasn't any happier about it, though for different reasons, telling Dez and Eva she'd arrived to a flooded basement, a power outage and a lineup of wet people. It seemed even a torrential downpour wasn't enough to keep the diehards away from the bar for a night, although Betty—selling what she could by cash and candlelight—was planning on breaking with tradition and closing early. That would keep anyone from getting too drunk and ensure the best chance everyone, including Betty herself, got home safely.

Dez wasn't sure if and when he and Eva would reach the same point but, for him at least, it wasn't happening unless Sully was with him.

They next headed to the two shelters Bulldog used the most. Both had already filled up for the night and there was no sign of the guy at either. Dez knew Bulldog well enough to appreciate he was smart about ensuring a roof over his head when needed. He was typically among those who arrived just as the night shelters were opening, ensuring himself the best chance at a bed. That Bulldog wasn't there either meant he'd found somewhere else to hole up or that he hadn't been able to get here.

Hoping for the former, Dez and Eva drove over to the house where they'd dropped Bulldog off last night. While they found his friend—a skinny ex-junkie everyone called Mouse—there was again no sign of Bulldog, despite the fact he'd left his stuff there.

Their last stop was The Hub which, while closed for the day in terms of programming, had remained open as a temporary emergency shelter. There, Dez and Eva found Myra Shingoose, Street Worker Exit Strategy director, lending a hand with cleaning the supper dishes.

"I haven't seen Bulldog since he left here earlier today with a young man he was with."

"Sullivan Gray," Dez said. "So neither of them's been back since?"

"No, sorry. Why? Is everything okay?"

Dez didn't feel like offering up a placating lie and so ignored the question. "If you see either of them, can you give Eva or me a call?"

"I'll do my best," Myra said. "Though I'm afraid I'm going to be stuck back here a while yet. Our soup kitchen manager left shortly after Bulldog and Sullivan, and he didn't return for the supper shift, so a few of us are working overtime here. I'm worried something might have happened to him."

"Maybe he just didn't bother coming back in," Eva said. "It's pretty crappy out there."

"No," Myra said. "It's not like him. He's one of our most reliable employees. Granted, he's been going a little off the rails lately, but that happens to everyone around here from time to time."

"Off the rails how?" Dez asked.

Myra stopped scrubbing a pot, swiping at a trickle of sweat on her forehead and focusing fully on her visitors. "He's been spending a lot of time with Sparrow lately, and I think it's likely he's developed some strong feelings for her. Bree was working hard with her, and had managed to get her into some programming here. Sparrow was taking well to it, was giving it her all. You have to understand, the programs we offer are intensive and, for those who throw themselves in the way Sparrow did, can become a 24/7 job. Thanks to Bree, Sparrow was making some real positive changes in her life. Zane—that's our soup kitchen manager, Zane Mazur—he found himself kind of left out in the cold with her for a while. She didn't have time for a relationship at that stage in the programming, and he didn't like that. But he adapted, and I think started to realize how important it was for Sparrow. Then Bree died. Sparrow spun back out into her old ways and Zane's been running after her ever since, trying to protect her."

"Do you think that's what he's doing now?" Eva asked. "Trying to protect Sparrow?"

"Maybe," Myra said. "Probably. I don't know. Maybe he got word about her location and went to get her. I know he's been trying to find her. Lots of people have said he's been asking around the past couple days, with no luck."

Dez offered Myra what he hoped was a reassuring smile. "Well, since Sully and Bulldog were looking for Sparrow, I'm hoping we'll find Sparrow and Zane when we locate our own guys. We'll make sure to keep you posted."

Back in the car with nowhere else to go besides The Forks, Eva tried all the phone numbers again, maintaining their run of bad luck on the communication front as Dez navigated around flooded streets and floating debris. Trees were coming apart in the wind and leaving pieces of themselves everywhere. People's outdoor belongings were blowing around and would likely never be reunited with the correct owner. And the power was still out, making it a challenge to see anything until you were damn near on top of it.

But it wasn't until they hit Forks Bridge that the situation went from bad to worse. Massive search lights had been rolled out to aid in what looked to be the evacuation of The Forks, and they illuminated a steady stream of traffic flowing across the bridge into Riverview. Across the river, the glow from additional search lights was just visible, suggesting other Forks residents were fleeing the island for the North Bank district.

Two patrol cars were stationed this side of Forks Bridge, ensuring as much order as possible.

"We're not allowing anyone else into The Forks tonight, sir," one of the officers said, his tone suggestive of a man who'd repeated the words umpteen times.

"Clark, it's me. Dez."

"Oh, hey. Sorry, I'm on autopilot." He leaned over further to see into the car. "Hi, Eva."

Eva waved as Dez continued to stare at the mass exodus of high-end cars. "The Forks is evacuating?"

"Yeah. Just got a call about half an hour ago. Engineers at the dam say it won't hold much longer, so they're going to need to do a controlled release soon. The Forks is going, one way or another, so everyone's being ordered to move to high land. There's even parts of North Bank, Riverview and New Town that are being told to evacuate."

"Shit," Dez said. "Listen, I know you've got your orders, but I need to get into The Forks."

"No one in, Dez. Sorry."

"Clark, my brother could be down there. I need to find him."

"Come on, Dez."

"Please."

Clark stared at Dez but finally heaved a sigh. "You go down there now, you're taking your life in your hands. The city has said it won't be held responsible for anyone who enters The Forks or refuses to leave. And the dam release is imminent, about an hour from now—just enough for us to get everyone and ourselves out."

Eva's voice sounded from beside him. "Dez."

"No, Eva."

"We can't. You know we can't. We've got Kayleigh to think of."

"But if Sully's down there—"

"That's a big if right now, Dez. Are you going to risk your life for an if? What would I tell Kayleigh if anything happened to you? And what would I tell Sully if it turns out he isn't down there? How do you think he'd feel if something happened to you because you were trying to find him? It would destroy him, Dez. You know it would. Look, Paul would have got the order to evacuate. Let's stay here for a few minutes and see if he comes across. Most of his family's properties are in New Town, right? He's likely to go there."

Dez stared back down at the darkness below where he knew The Forks sat, at risk of disappearing entirely beneath the flood. There was still a chance Sully was down there somewhere, but Eva was right. The chances were greater right now that Kayleigh would be down one parent if Dez went into The Forks—and for no good reason if it turned out Sully wasn't even there. "Yeah. Yeah, okay. We'll keep an eye out from here."

Eva's hand found his in the ambient glow from the search lights and the steady stream of headlights, eased white knuckles from the steering wheel. "I'm sorry, Dez. I'm so sorry."

Dez gently squeezed her fingers but said nothing in response. His attention was focused on those cars, on the faces of their drivers just visible in the glare of the takedown lights the two police cruisers were using to help guide traffic. If he kept his attention there, Dez hoped it wouldn't stray across the bridge, to the portion of the city lying on the edge of destruction.

Because deep down, he knew that's exactly where Sully was.

17

Sully suspected the bus he'd caught into The Forks close to an hour ago was among the last of the night.

And, if the string of cars and the panicked rush in driveways was anything to go by, it might well have been one of the last buses down here, full stop.

The bus had gotten him across the river and partway east on Oldwater Road, but that particular route circled back before reaching the portion of The Forks where Paul Dunsmore lived. Sully ended up walking what he estimated to be a kilometre or two the rest of the way, relying on memory as he pieced together the path he and Dez had taken earlier.

He was typically skilled at navigation, and it didn't let him down now. Through rain and the dark, he made his way through largely deserted streets and past eerily silent homes.

While his sight was limited to the ghosts of those who died violently, he knew there were many, many others he couldn't see. He could sense them now, could feel their eyes on him, silent sentinels in this abandoned neighbourhood. They crowded him; here, on this lonely dark stretch of roadway, he had proven easy to find. A beacon, Marc Echoles had called him, someone with an aura so bright he'd never be able to hide from them. He picked up the pace instead, breaking into a run as he sought to put both rain and spirit behind him.

Paul Dunsmore's house was a refuge at the end of the journey, standing silently, just visible through the gates and the driving rain as Sully pressed the button next to the speaker. As seconds ticked by without response, it occurred to him it was likely Paul had joined the mass exodus from The Forks—naturally providing yet another warning to Sully he should be doing the same.

He was stopped by the image that formed just the other side of the gate, crystallizing through the downpour. Bloodless bound hands reached out to him, purple petals peeking between fingers. Eyes, seemingly unseeing, fixed on him through strings of hair. From the shrub next to her—one of two planted just the other side of the gate—a small flock of birds broke through and flew toward the blackened sky. Sully didn't think he needed to be an expert to conclude they had been sparrows.

"I'm not going anywhere, okay?" he told Breanna.

There was still no response on the speaker. It was possible Paul had left, of course, but it occurred to Sully it might also mean the box was affected by the power outage. Tall brick walls stood either side, wrapping around the property, and Sully took the one to the right, planting a booted foot along the edge and trying to push off to grab at the top ledge. His foot slipped and he succeeded in nothing but banging a knee.

He cursed and rubbed at the injury, but didn't allow himself long before taking a running start at the wall and leaping at it. This time, he kicked off the wall with one foot, propelling him upward until he could grasp the top in his hands. The ledge was slippery with moisture but he managed to hold to it, fighting for purchase with his feet until he could catch a gap between the bricks with the toe of one boot. Using his arms, he pulled himself up and over, managing to land on his feet on the other side.

He sprinted toward the house and was most of the way there before a flash of lightning exposed the river, no longer high on the low-rising bank, but partway up the house. There was no way

Paul was here, no way he could possibly have stayed given what Sully was seeing. He could hear the crash of waves along the west side of the building as the high river pummelled it, and the occasional crack of something more substantial washing hard into the wall. Sully had seen images on the news in other cities hit hard by flood, remembered pictures of houses forced from foundations and tossed apart like elementary school popsicle stick projects. If Paul was still here, he wasn't merely stupid, he was suicidal. Sully would be no better if he didn't turn tail and get the hell out of here now.

And yet, as he took another few steps forward and squinted through the rain, he could make out the image of Breanna's pale form in the window, hands outstretched to him, one index finger beckoning him forward.

One other possibility occurred to Sully, one that had him running to the door. If Paul knew something, and he'd intended to pass it along to Sully, who was to say someone else hadn't been made aware? What if the killer had been here, had gone after Paul? If so, the guy could be in serious trouble right now and facing a greater immediate threat than just the flood waters.

The unlocked front door confirmed Sully's fears.

Inside, his boots creating a muddy path on the already-wet floor, Sully called out Paul's name. While the storm was raging outside, the soundproofed walls were holding—for now—enabling him to quickly ascertain there was no response. He moved on to the other side of the house, finding the kitchen where he and Dez had visited the man yesterday. He called again but was met by only silence.

With only the lightning and the glow from Marc's flashlight to go by, Sully contemplated the mammoth task before him. It was a big house and there was little time to search it, the river reaching near the halfway point on the sliding glass doors and—if that creaking sound he kept hearing was any indication—threatening to burst through and flood much of the entire main floor.

Breanna was standing next to him now, close enough he could

sense the emotion she was unable to show in a physical way. She was afraid, the urgency rolling off her in waves that rivalled the violence of the river.

"Where?" he asked, and she disappeared only to show herself to him along the opposite wall of the kitchen. He followed until he saw her standing, staring at a closed door.

Slogging over, Sully tested the door next to her and found it unlocked. Behind it, made visible by the beam from the flashlight, lay a set of stairs leading down and into an estimated three feet of water.

"Great," Sully muttered, his brain wandering into places he didn't want to explore. It was just possible he would find something down there he didn't want to see. But, up here, the intensity Breanna was emitting made Sully wonder if she wouldn't shove him down the stairs if he didn't start moving. He took the first few steps, gritting his teeth as he waded into the flood-made pool. He'd hoped his sodden clothes and the fact he'd spent most of the past couple of days soaked from rain or submerged in river water would prepare him, but the cold still bit into him as he waded into waist-deep water, searching for Sparrow in the darkness.

He considered calling out again, but something stopped him, the silence too stifling and strong to cut through.

And, as it happened, there was no need.

Paul's body was floating along the nearest wall, facedown in the water.

Sully slogged toward him, splashing through the flooded basement until he could gain the other man's side. He grunted as he strained to turn the man over, to draw his face back to the air. But it seemed any help Sully had hoped to provide would be in vain. Paul's face, illuminated in the white light of the flashlight beam, was pale and still, his eyes open just a crack, just enough to see they were fixed yet unfocused. Sully fumbled for a pulse at the man's throat, but his hand was shaking too badly and his fingers too numb to find the confirmation he was looking for.

Cold dread crawled over Sully as he stared down at the death-still man, wondering how he'd ended up this way. But now wasn't the time for a fact-finding mission. Only one thing needed checked, and Sully found it as he drew up the sleeve of Paul's sweater.

There, on the inner right arm, was a dripping, lit black candle.

"What the hell?" he muttered into the darkness, his brain turning over this latest find. The tattoo was in the right location and was etched into otherwise clean skin—identical to Marc's and the one on the man who had killed Breanna and Gabriella. The why was another question, one for which Sully knew he might never find an answer, not with Paul dead and having taken any knowledge with him.

For now, there was only one thing left to sort out. He needed to search the house for Sparrow and get out of here before they all ended up like Paul.

Sully started to wade away from the body when a noise had him pulling up short. It was the sound of someone coughing.

It definitely hadn't come from Paul.

Sully turned from the body and moved toward a hallway, having to shove hard against the nearest door to move it through the water. Again, he heard the cough, this time closer.

He scanned the room with with his light and felt his heart thud against his chest wall as he caught the image of Bulldog sitting slumped in a high-backed chair, water already up to his chest.

Sloshing over, Sully grasped the older man's face in his free hand.

"Bulldog?" he asked, his voice starting to exhibit the same chilled shakes as the rest of him. "Can you hear me? Talk to me, man."

Bulldog's eyes fluttered open, and Sully angled the flashlight to allow the other man to identify his rescuer. His voice, when it came, was sluggish. "Sully?"

Sully huffed out a relieved breath. "Yeah, man. It's me. We need to get out of here."

"Gonna be hard."

"Why?"

"Think I'm tied to a chair."

Sully reached below the water's surface and found one of Bulldog's hands. Feeling further, he came to a wrist and a thin, smooth band circling it. Zip ties.

Praying his pocketknife hadn't shaken or washed free since he'd left Marc's earlier, Sully felt around in the hoodie pocket next to the plastic bag containing his phone. When his fingers settled over the knife casing, he let loose a short bark of laughter.

"Yeah, good job, kid," Bulldog said, voice sounding clearer than it had moments ago. "Now cut me loose so we can find Sparrow and get the hell out of here."

Sully located the knife blade and pulled it free after three tries with frozen fingers. "Paul's dead. Did you get a look at the guy who attacked you?"

"No. I assumed it was Paul. You sure he's dead?"

Sully tucked the flashlight under his arm as he went to work on the ties around Bulldog's wrists, struggling to stifle the cold-induced tremble in his hands. "He was floating facedown in the water. He looked pretty dead to me."

"How'd that happen?"

"No idea, man. I didn't have time for an autopsy."

"So if he's dead, who the hell hit me then?"

"I don't know. What are you doing here anyway?"

"Zane Mazur. You met him at the Hub."

"The kitchen manager? Yeah, I met him."

"He told me he saw Bree having a heated talk with Paul shortly before she was murdered, didn't know about what. But it got me thinking maybe Paul knew more than he was saying. Then Zane told me Paul took Sparrow—that someone saw him and a couple goons grabbing her a couple days ago. Zane and me, we came here to find her and to get her out. We took the bus out here and we were buzzed through the gate. Weird thing was, the front door was unlocked, and there was no sign of Paul. We just walked in and started looking."

Sully succeeded in slicing through the first of the zip ties and started on the second. "Where's Zane now?"

"No idea. Maybe the same person who clobbered me got him, too. Coulda been Paul, I guess."

"But you never saw Paul?"

"Nope, but then I didn't get a look at the guy who whacked me. Zane and I split up to search for Sparrow, though, so it's possible Zane ran into him. If so, it's probably not a good thing. I was in the basement having a look around when I got cracked on the head."

"So no sign of Sparrow then?"

"I didn't get much chance to look."

"So why did you think Paul would have had something to do with Sparrow's disappearance?"

"I don't know. Why does any man take a young girl?"

Sully managed to cut the second of the zip ties securing Bulldog's wrists. "Not Paul. He plays for the other team."

"So maybe he's bi."

"Maybe .... Don't tell me your feet are tied too?"

"Sorry, kid."

Sully grimaced as he squatted down to feel below the surface for the ties, holding his breath as the water lapped around his nose. Bulldog's assailant had been clever, securing his shins above the crossbar rather than his ankles to the chair's base, ensuring the prisoner couldn't simply lean back to free his legs.

Working blind and with increasingly numbed fingers, Sully moved slowly, but finally felt the snap as one tie released.

"Almost there. Just get me out of here, and we'll find Sparrow and leave."

Sully lifted himself up far enough to respond. "We don't know for sure she's here."

"She's here. I know it. I don't know why, but I just—Sully, behind you!"

Sully turned, the flashlight still clutched under his arm moving with him until it illuminated the form of Zane Mazur standing in the doorway, an industrial-strength flashlight in one hand.

"Jesus Christ, Maze," Bulldog said. "Thank Christ. I thought someone got you, too."

"He tried. But I got to Paul first."

The reason for Paul's death became clearer. "Did you kill him?"

"No choice. It was him or me. He already killed Breanna, and God knows what he's done to Sparrow."

Using what light was available, Sully scanned the faces of the two other men. "Why is it the two of you think Paul brought Sparrow here?"

"Someone just told me he and a couple guys grabbed her recently," Zane said. "I haven't been able to get that confirmed, but it was enough to bring me here to see for myself. Look, just trust me on this, okay? She's here somewhere. I know it. You need to help me find her."

Sully wasn't satisfied, but there would be time for more questions as they searched the house. He returned his attention to Bulldog, dropping back fully into the cold water to sever the last of the zip ties.

Zane beckoned impatiently from the doorway. "Let's go."

"Give me a minute," Bulldog said as Sully dragged him to standing. "I can barely feel my feet."

"It's partially from the cold," Sully said. "Lean on me and go slow. Not much option with all this water, anyway. Movement will get the blood flowing."

Sully took a good portion of Bulldog's not-insignificant weight as they made to follow the other man. As Zane turned, Sully spotted a nickel-plated handgun tucked into the waistband of his jeans, just visible above the rising water, its handle propping up his jacket in the back.

Apparently it hadn't been lost on Bulldog. "Jesus, Maze, where'd you get a gun?"

"Dunsmore had it on him," Zane said. "He tried to kill me with it, but I beat him to the punch."

Sully hadn't seen any gunshot wounds on Paul, but that didn't mean they weren't there. The man's clothing and the fact he'd been floating in water could easily conceal gunshot wounds until someone had a chance to look closer.

"I'm still not seeing what motive Paul would have for taking Sparrow," Sully said.

"Seriously?" Zane said as he led them into the hallway and further back into the basement. "She's gorgeous. Find me a man who wouldn't think about taking her."

"Well, there's Paul for starters," Sully said. "He was gay."

Zane angled his face slightly toward Sully for a moment but otherwise kept going. "What the hell are you talking about? He was always hanging around women."

"Maybe he just liked hanging out with them," Sully said.

"Or maybe he swings both ways," Zane said. "Look, I'm telling you Sparrow's here somewhere. I just need to find her."

Sully couldn't fully disagree, not with Breanna standing at the end of the hallway, dead stare fixed on them as they approached. When Sully made eye contact, she lifted her arm and pointed left.

"Right or left?" Zane asked, and Sully—his focus having been entirely on Breanna—noticed they'd come to a T-intersection in the hall.

"Left," he said.

"How do you know?"

"I have a feeling," Sully said.

Zane wasn't sold, and Sully wasn't about to reveal the reason for his own certainty.

"Look, you go left and I'll take the right," Zane said. "We'll cover more ground that way."

He didn't wait for a response before swinging the beam of his flashlight around and taking off in the direction it now pointed, leaving Sully and Bulldog with the other path.

Bulldog had been largely quiet but he chose that moment to speak up, the tremor in his voice sounding like it was caused by more than just the cold. "Uh, Sully? Wasn't Paul's body floating down at the other end of the hall when we came out of the room a minute ago?"

Sully spun, the pull of the water nearly throwing him off-balance. He put out a hand, catching himself against the wall as he trained the flashlight on the spot where he'd found the floating corpse.

Paul was gone.

18

SULLY'S first thought was to figure out where Paul had disappeared to.

While the currents outside were intense, it was too calm where they were for a body to have simply drifted away.

Sully took a step toward the area where he'd last seen Paul, but was stopped by a hand on his arm.

"Sully, no," Bulldog said. "There's no time."

Bulldog had a point. The water, previously at the level of his waist, was now closer to the base of Sully's ribcage. All the effort put into the planning and construction of this house was not enough to protect it from the forces of nature, and the Kimotan was proving to be an intruder the Dunmores hadn't considered.

Sully was six feet tall, Bulldog just a few inches shorter. And Sparrow, by all accounts, was tiny enough to make both of them resemble grizzlies in comparison. If the water was reaching uncomfortable heights for Sully, he didn't want to consider what that meant for her if she was trapped down here somewhere.

Breanna had moved further down the hall to the left and was waiting on them, so Sully gave up on Paul and headed in the direction the ghost was laying out for him. Now that they were all in one location, Sully was hopeful Breanna would be able to take them where they needed to go.

She was standing in front of a door at the end of the hall, a solid piece of steel given the appearance of regular hardwood but for the industrial handle. Sully tried it, but found it locked.

"Is there a key?" he asked Breanna.

Bulldog's voice was shaking with cold as he answered. "Is Bree here?"

"Yeah. She's showing me this is the door, but we can't get through it."

"Maybe Paul's got it."

The water splashed around Sully's torso as he jumped at the sound of a voice from their left. "Paul's got it, all right."

Sully met the approaching glow of a flashlight with his own beam, illuminating a figure coming toward them. If Bulldog wasn't also staring right at the image of Paul Dunsmore, Sully would have thought he was seeing another ghost.

"What the hell?" Bulldog said. "We thought you were dead."

Paul moved past them, fumbling with a set of keys until he found one that fit a small box to the side of the door. "In my spare time, I act with the Kimotan Rapids Stratford Society—and, yes, I'm well aware of the stereotype of gay men and theatre. Last year, I played the ghost of Hamlet's father. I learned how to play dead."

Behind the box was a PIN pad, and the door beeped open after Paul keyed in four digits.

A short hallway beyond, revealed once they heaved open the door, was flooded torso-deep with water.

"Oh, sweet Jesus, no," Paul moaned. "It's supposed to be airtight in here. There's oxygen pumped in, of course. It's the outer chamber of a panic room."

"Is Sparrow in there?" Sully asked.

Paul nodded. "Behind the door ahead. The main room is behind it."

He started slogging toward the door which, unfortunately for him, left him ill-prepared for an attack by Bulldog even Sully didn't see coming. Bulldog took as large a leap as the water would allow, throwing himself at the other man's back and taking the pair of them beneath the surface.

Sully played the flashlight's beam along the water, searching for a sign of the submerged men. At least one of them would have to come up eventually and, seconds later, it was Bulldog whose head and shoulders reappeared. One meaty hand followed, fingers bunched up in Paul's sweater and dragging him forward to meet the force of Bulldog's opposite fist.

Bulldog punched Paul twice in the face, his hold on his clothing all that prevented the man from falling back into the water. The shorter man was winding up for another punch when he appeared to change his mind, hand stilling mid-air before joining the other in the soaked folds of Paul's sweater.

Bulldog forced a stunned Paul beneath the water's surface, the tension on Bulldog's face and the flailing of the other man's arms providing all the evidence Sully needed as to what his friend intended.

Sully pushed forward until he could lay a restraining grip on Bulldog's arms—or as much as he could manage with the flashlight still clutched in one hand.

"Let him go, Bulldog! Don't do this!"

Sully's position had the beam of the light shining directly up into Bulldog's face, and it revealed a mask of rage. There would be no reasoning with the man.

Paul was still struggling, but he was weakening.

Sully didn't give a damn about Paul, but he did care about Bulldog. The man had lived a hard life but, as far as Sully knew, he'd never killed anyone. If they got out of this in one piece, the last thing Sully wanted for his friend was life imprisonment in a six-by-eight cell.

He did the only thing he could think; he delivered as solid a punch as he could manage with frozen fingers to the side of Bulldog's face.

The blow had the desired effect—to a point. Bulldog released Paul. Then he came at Sully.

Sully felt his back collide with a nearby wall and Bulldog's knuckles pressing into his chest as he held him there.

"Bulldog—"

"Don't you fucking protect him! He doesn't deserve it!"

"I'm not trying to protect him. I'm trying to protect *you*."

"I don't need it. Sparrow needs it! My sister needed it!"

"Your sister?"

"He killed her! He killed Bree!"

"What the hell are you talking about?" The voice had Bulldog turning his head to where the dull ambient light from the flashlight revealed an exhausted Paul standing, slightly hunched, in the water as he regarded them. The question had been spoken through heaving breaths and now he broke off into a round of watery coughs.

Bulldog's voice was a growl. "I'll finish you, you sick bastard."

"Bulldog, no!" Sully grabbed at his friend's shirt in a weak effort to keep him from returning to Paul. Breanna was back, had positioned herself in front of Paul, dead stare focused on her brother.

"Give me one reason."

Sully answered quietly, hoping Paul wouldn't hear above his continued coughing. "Breanna doesn't want it. She's standing between you and Paul. You'll have to go through her to get to him."

Bulldog stilled and, in the seconds that passed, Paul regained control of his breathing, enabling him to answer the accusation. "I didn't kill Bree. She was my friend. I cared about her."

"So if it wasn't you, who did it?"

"I thought it was Danny. But, now—" The sound of sloshing water from the door to the panic room's outer chamber redirected his attention. "—I think you're better off asking him."

Sully had trained the light on the doorway in the same moment, allowing them to spot Zane Mazur standing there, arms extended, his own flashlight bathing the small room in additional light. The gun, previously in the waistband of his pants, was now in his hand.

"You're a slippery one, Paulie. I really thought I'd killed you. Didn't see the bullet wounds, but the way you flew back when I fired, the way your face looked …. Wow."

Bulldog looked back and forth between Zane and Paul. "What the hell is going on here?"

Paul squinted into the light from Zane's flashlight. "What do you say, man? Want to enlighten everyone?"

"Fuck you, Paul."

Paul wasn't giving up that easily. "Honestly, until you showed up tonight, I thought Echoles killed Gabby and that Bree was murdered by her husband. But it was all actually you. I knew you were gaga for Gabby and were pissed she was into the professor instead. But why Bree? And why are you after Sparrow?"

"Gabby?" Sully asked. "You mean Gabriella Aguado?"

"Yeah," Paul said. "You saw my tattoo. Zane's got one just like it. So did Gabby and the prof."

"Was anyone not in this coven?" Bulldog asked. Then, "We're wasting time here. We need to get to Sparrow."

"She's safer where she is, right now," Paul said. "So how about it, Zane? What's the story? Gabby didn't shower you with adoration, so you took her out?"

"Echoles changed her, and I hated she was letting him. She was this wild thing and he was trying to tame her, to mold her into something resembling the dead wife he never got over. She resisted him for a while, but she was starting to change. She wasn't interested in the same things anymore."

"The drugs, you mean," Paul said. "A lot of us weren't into that garbage you were peddling for Ken Barwell."

"She was," Zane said. "Or at least she used to be. We'd trip for hours, the two of us. We'd sit up all night together, giggling like kids or just staring into each other's eyes and reading each other's thoughts. I spent my whole life looking for someone I could trust.

She was the closest thing I ever found to family. You know what that's like, to have the only family you've ever known pulled away from you?"

A growl sounded low in Bulldog's throat, but he didn't charge, his gaze shifting between the two men in front of him. Bulldog, Sully realized, knew exactly what it was to have your only family taken; the only thing saving Breanna's killer from facing his wrath was the fact he was trying to figure out which of them it was.

For Sully's part, he could now see the answer. It was there, in the way Breanna was now circling Zane, staring as if seeing him for the first time as he truly was. She hadn't seen his face the night she died, but she recognized the darkness inside him.

"I'm sure you're aware I was caught breaking into the professor's house," Zane continued. "I got up to his altar, figured I'd do him in with his own athame. But that bastard's tougher than he looks, put up a good fight. So I ran. Police caught up with me not far from there, knife still in my hand."

The break-in at Marc Echoles's house. Sully had never looked to see who had been behind it, figured it was more or less just some stupid drunk prank. He was kicking himself for that now.

Zane wasn't done, but the spite left his voice momentarily as he spoke about the woman he'd professed to love. "I broke in there right after what happened with Gabby. I blamed him for it, wanted him to pay."

"You mean after you killed her," Sully said.

"I didn't kill her. She got high and jumped."

"She wasn't using anymore. You drugged her, you got her to that bridge and you made sure she stepped over that railing. Then you choked her until she pulled her hands from the railing so when you let go, she had nothing to hold onto. She didn't jump. She fell. And the only reason she fell was because you made it happen. You murdered her, Zane."

Zane's face, in the glow of Sully's flashlight, slackened. "How the hell do you know that?"

"And all this time I thought it was Marc," Paul said. "He was so angry after it happened, refused to talk about her. He was so sure he'd turned her around, that she was done with the drugs and that wild life. He seemed really let down when we all heard she jumped off a bridge with a system full of acid—so let down by her being back on the drugs that I figured he might have even been pissed off enough to have killed her."

"Echoles doesn't have it in him to do something like that," Zane said. "He's too fucking soft to do what needs to be done."

"And Bree?" Paul asked. "Something needed doing there too, huh? I mean, I knew she didn't like you, that she was suspicious about your intentions with Sparrow. She'd started to think of Sparrow as a daughter, begged me to look after the girl, to make sure she was protected. Figured I had the money and the connections to help her disappear. God help me, I didn't believe Bree about just how evil you were. I knew things weren't so great between her and Danny, that he was struggling to stay sober, and I started to wonder whether she might be too. But she wasn't. She was a hell of a lot more on the ball than I was, and I can't help thinking she'd still be here if I'd just listened. Because Danny didn't kill her, did he? You did."

"She always had to stick her nose into other people's business."

Bulldog's anger found its target. "That's what she did to help people, you asshole. She made other people's problems her own."

"She did it one too many times."

Bulldog's snarl became a roar, and it was only Sully's shove—nearly sending the shorter man backwards into the water—that kept him from charging Zane and the gun he had levelled in their direction.

"She was his sister," Sully explained, hoping that might be enough to prevent Zane's shooting Bulldog now that he'd regained his balance.

"I'm sorry about that. You can believe me or not. I don't care. But she didn't leave me any choice."

"You'd better fucking explain that to me, you bastard! You owe me at least that much!"

Zane, it seemed, couldn't argue that point. "It started with Ken Barwell. I knew him through the Black Candle, and he offered to set me up in business to help me get through university. I love The Hub; it's like home. But the pay is shit. So I started selling for Barwell, and I was turning a good profit. Only I discovered pretty quick what kind of scum he was when he attacked Abby, one of the girls I was looking after. I decided I was going to screw him over, hit him where it hurt. Figured if I played my cards right, I'd get him out of the picture and get my hands on his stock."

"The drugs?" Paul asked.

"And the guns. There's a good market for them. Barwell gets his supply—drugs and guns—from a major player out west, and Ken regularly owes the guy huge stacks of cash. I figured if I got ahold of his stash, it was only a matter of time before his supplier came at him for money Ken couldn't get his hands on. In the drug world, that means you end up stuffed in a trunk and taken somewhere for a conversation with a baseball bat or a shotgun. Only I couldn't get close enough."

Sully thought back to that tense conversation with Ken Barwell as Bulldog provided the conclusion. "Sparrow ripped him off for you."

"He wanted at her in the worst way afterward," Zane said. "She knew it and she was scared. I told her I'd protect her, but she went to Bree instead. She told her all about the rip-off and the fact Barwell was out to get her."

"And Bree came to me asking for the money to pay off Ken," Paul said. "She told me what Sparrow did, and asked me to act as a go-between. I reluctantly agreed and did what I could to smooth things over. Ken agreed to let Sparrow go once the money was paid, but he wanted another condition met. He wanted the name of the man who sent Sparrow to rip him off. And Bree knew, didn't she? She figured out it was you."

"She was going to rat me out to Barwell. I had no choice. I had to keep her from telling. Do you have any idea what Barwell would have done to me had he found out?"

Sully put an arm out in front of Bulldog to act as a restraint. If Bulldog so chose, he could shove right past but he stayed where he was, allowing the exchange to continue between the two coven members. Because, come right down to it, that conversation was all that was keeping that door open and preventing Zane from adding to his kill list.

"You're not only a coward, Mazur, you're an idiot too," Paul said. "Bree and I had a big blowup right before she was killed over whether or not to provide your name to Barwell. But I'm the one who wanted to identify you. She wouldn't hear of it. Bree said she couldn't live with having your blood on her hands when Barwell came for you. She asked me to look after Sparrow instead, to help her disappear from both Barwell and from you. I never thought in a million years you were capable of murder. I knew Danny Newton's history so, when Bree turned up dead, I just figured it was a domestic homicide like they were saying. Had I known how right Bree was about what kind of scumbag you were, I would have figured out a way to hide her from you, too."

"I didn't want to kill her, and I honestly didn't think I could go through with it," Zane said. "I was watching her that night, trying to figure out a plan when I saw her husband smacking her around inside the house. She was a mess when she left, and I followed her for a minute or two until I figured no one was around to see. Then I gave her a good crack on the head. I got her back to my car, tied her up and took her to one of those empty Riverview houses.

"I didn't think I could finish it. With Gabby, it happened so fast. She just basically slipped through my fingers and was gone. With Breanna, it was going to have to be deliberate. I had to psyche myself up to it. She started to wake up, though, and I don't know why, but the thought of her looking at me, seeing me doing it, it freaked me out. So I just did it as quick as I could. I meant to take her back home after, dump her next to her drunk husband for the cops to find, but in the end, I just left her there."

An enraged roar tore from Bulldog's throat, Zane saved only by the hindrances to the shorter man's movements in the form of deep water and Sully. Even so, it was all Sully could manage to hold his friend back.

He spoke quietly to Bulldog, his back to Zane as he relied on his friend to be his eyes. "Bulldog, no. He'll shoot you. You think Bree wants that?"

"Bree's dead!"

"She's here, man. She's right here, beside you. Don't, okay? Please. Just don't."

Bulldog was heaving breaths like a man who'd just run five blocks flat out. His eyes, fixed on Zane with a hate Sully had never known in Bulldog, finally shifted away from his sister's killer and settled on his friend, enabling Sully to witness the gradual return of sanity.

"Where is she?"

Sully nodded to Bulldog's left, where Breanna stood, lifting her hands toward her brother's face, fingers reaching out as if to touch his jaw.

Bulldog's voice was a whisper. "I'm sorry I couldn't protect you, Bree. I'm so sorry." Then he returned his glare to Zane. "If you think I'm letting you leave here with Sparrow, you're dead wrong. You've got a max seven rounds in that thing with one chambered. There are three of us and you'll need all seven just to stop me."

Sully turned in time to see Zane trying for a smirk, the expression of a man who was only just finding his legs as a killer and was trying to look the part. "Leave with her? I don't want to leave with her. I came here to kill her. You've just made it easy for me. I thought she and I were going to be something but your sister got to her first. I'll tell you something, man. I'm finally starting to figure it out. No bitch is worth this hassle. You can have her. She's all yours. You can all go to hell together."

He stepped back and, before any of the others could reach the door through the relentless tug of water, he'd sealed them inside.

19

SULLY AND PAUL pushed water aside to reach the door, Paul moving to unlock the PIN pad box this side of the panic room's entrance.

He'd just got it open when they heard a pair of gunshots from the other side, the sound dulled by steel and solid wood.

Sully wasn't surprised when Paul's efforts to key in the combination came up empty.

Paul slammed his palm against the wall. "The bastard must have shot out the mechanism."

"And there's no other way to unlock the door?" Sully asked. "Nothing we can trip?"

"If it were that easy, it wouldn't be a very good panic room, now, would it?"

Bulldog had found another problem, busy shoving against the door behind which Paul was keeping Sparrow. "Forget that door. Help me with this one! The water's too high and, if that little girl's in it, she could be drowning!"

Sully didn't bother sharing the obvious: that even if they got Sparrow out of the room, she'd drown with them regardless. Even so, there was something to be said for the comfort of having someone with you when you went, and the thought of the teenager being stuck back there alone wasn't right. Sure, Breanna would no doubt be with her—the ghost had disappeared the moment Zane sealed them in here—but chances were Sparrow wouldn't know that. Nor was it likely to make her feel a whole lot better if someone told her she was trapped back there with a dead woman.

Paul joined Bulldog at the door, pulling a set of keys from his pocket and holding them in front of his flashlight until he could find a particular one.

Bulldog turned heated eyes on Paul. "Why do you keep the door locked?"

"The room was designed for the possibility of intruders. It locks from either side with a key. My father had this idea that if someone chased him into the panic room's outer chamber, he could either barricade himself in the inner one until help arrived, or lock the intruder in there. He's nothing if not paranoid."

"I meant, why do you have Sparrow locked in there?"

"I told you, I made a promise to Bree to look after her. I've been trying to keep that promise."

"By holding her against her will?"

Paul took the keys below the water's surface, presumably to unlock the door. "It turned out it wasn't just Barwell or Zane she needed protecting from. She'd become her own worst enemy."

Any further explanation was prevented by Paul's exclamation of, "What the hell?"

Bulldog's eyes fell from Paul's face to the water, as if he could see what it was bugging the other man if he focused in hard enough. "What the hell, what?"

"I've unlocked it. I mean, the handle's moving back and forth all right. But the door won't open."

Bulldog pushed Paul aside with more force than was likely necessary. "Let me at it."

He shoved, then shouldered the door, putting as much force into it as the barrier of water would allow. The door didn't budge.

With nothing else working, all three men lined up, Bulldog

and Sully putting their shoulders to the task while Paul reached between them to push. Sully felt the door shudder slightly, but otherwise there was no indication the force was accomplishing anything except bruises for the three of them.

Bulldog grabbed Paul's flashlight and cast its beam into the seams and corners of the doorway, as if looking for the source of the problem. "I don't get this."

Paul had an idea—but it turned out to be one nobody wanted to hear. "Could be the water pressure's too uneven. If the other room's filled up, we won't be able to budge the door until it's the same our side."

Bulldog redirected the glare of the flashlight full into Paul's face, making the other man flinch and turn his head away. "Don't you even say something like that."

Why his brain picked this moment to recall it, Sully didn't know, but he found himself flashing back on a recent moment in his apartment above the bar, to a trapped bird and a ghost with a flower cupped within bound hands. Dez had been standing right outside, unable to enter what had, only moments before, been an unlocked and open door. Breanna had done it, had kept the door shut and sealed, trapping Sully in there with her until she could deliver her message to him.

And, suddenly, Sully saw another possibility.

"Paul? You said the room's supposed to be airtight, right?"

"Yeah, like this one. There's a setup to allow oxygen in but it's supposed to be safe in there from fire, flood and any other natural disaster. Obviously, my parents should be looking for a refund."

"Maybe they don't need one." Sully pressed an ear to the door, listening. "Sparrow? Can you hear me? Sparrow, please, if you can, answer me, okay?"

The reply was dull and muffled, but it was there. "What?"

Bulldog gave a quick bark of laughter. "God, it's good to hear your voice, kid!"

Sully flattened out a hand, motioning it toward the ground in a call for quiet. "Is there any water in there? Any flooding?"

"No! Get me the hell out of here! Now!"

Sully met Paul's eye. "Looks like the room's holding, after all."

"So why can't we get it open? All the pressure's on our side."

Sully didn't answer immediately, searching for the right words. Bulldog had no similar reservations.

"You think Bree's keeping the door sealed, don't you?"

Sully shrugged, ignoring the raised eyebrow and bemused expression Paul had turned on Bulldog. "She's capable of it. And she knows it's flooding out here. All of this, bringing us here, it's all been about protecting Sparrow, about saving her. I think she's still trying to do that."

"What are you two talking about?"

Bulldog granted Paul a glance. "Long story. And you probably wouldn't believe it, anyway. Just re-lock the door."

Sully didn't bother explaining to Paul, who was doing as Bulldog asked. The dull thuds of pounding fists on solid steel and muffled yelling suggested Sparrow wasn't so easily convinced.

Sully tried shouting back, but thought it likely she hadn't heard him above the sounds of her own protests.

He turned to Bulldog. "You try. Tell her it's flooding this side. She's better off staying in there until we can figure a way out of here."

Bulldog did as asked. "Sparrow, it's Bulldog, from The Hub! I'm Bree's brother! The water's really high this side, so we're going to leave you in there for now, all right?"

"Bulldog?" came the muffled reply. "Please, let me out!"

"I can't! Not yet! Soon, okay?"

It said something, whether for the level of trust Sparrow had in Bulldog or in Bree, that Sparrow quieted, the sounds of thumping and yelling stopping.

Sully and Paul had, in the meantime, worked their way to the other end of the short hall, Sully shining a light so Paul could examine the keypad. Using the tip of Sully's knife, Paul set to unscrewing the faceplate in the hopes a solution lay beneath.

There were a few minutes for questions, and Sully took advantage. "You said you were trying to protect Sparrow from herself. What did you mean?"

"Sparrow more or less went off the radar after Bree was killed. She fell back into drugs pretty heavy. I couldn't find her, but neither could Ken, so there was that at least. When I finally caught up to her, she was a mess, from both drugs and grief. Bree had really been sorting Sparrow out but, after she died, and with Danny Newton in jail for the murder, it was like Sparrow lost her will to stay straight. It wasn't just the coke anymore with her. She was getting into meth. Bringing her here has been as much about getting her clean as keeping her safe from Ken. She isn't exactly a willing participant in the detox, which is why I've had to keep her locked in. Then the weather situation went from bad to nightmare, and now I don't know what to do."

"Well, stating the obvious, the first thing we gotta do is get all four of us the hell outta here," Bulldog said. He'd spoken the words as much to Paul as to Sully, a clear sign his opinion about the businessman had changed.

Despite the peril of the situation, Sully found himself smiling. But it didn't last long. Sparrow hadn't, after all, needed saving from Paul. She'd needed protecting from Ken and Zane and from the rising river that was threatening to wash them into the next life. And while they'd found her, Sully was fully aware they hadn't succeeded in saving Sparrow from anything.

Not yet, anyway.

Paul was fiddling with the exposed mechanism, the keypad's faceplate left to dangle from a series of wires.

"It's no use," he finally grumbled. "I don't know my way around this sort of technology. I had a hard enough time installing my entertainment system."

Sully looked elsewhere for the answer. "Breanna, is there any way you can get this door open?"

She materialized next to him, focusing on the door before disappearing entirely. Sully waited, hoping, holding his breath as he waited for the click of a releasing lock.

But none came.

"Does someone want to tell me what's going on here?" Paul asked again. He faced Bulldog. "Why is he talking to Bree? He does mean our Bree, right?"

"Yeah, he means our Bree. Sully?"

Sully sighed, no point holding back on the truth now. Given he was likely going to be spending the rest of his life with these people, they might as well get to know one another. "Go ahead."

Bulldog provided the explanation. "Sully sees the dead, or at least the ones who die in bad ways like Bree did. They come to him for help. Bree wanted him to find Sparrow, to save her."

"From me?" Paul's voice was just one step above a whisper.

"From Mazur probably. From this flood. Maybe even from herself. She dedicated herself to helping girls who she saw as going down the same bad path she once travelled. And when she found out who Sparrow was, she would have taken her as a daughter. Bree never had kids of her own, so she would have gone all in with that girl."

While Bulldog had been explaining, Sully was playing the flashlight beam along the frame of the door, searching for potential weak spots. There didn't seem to be anything they'd be able to break through, but his eyes did settle on a large crack at the upper left corner, one that extended along part of the top of the steel door frame and then up toward the ceiling. It explained how it was the water had flowed into this otherwise airtight chamber; Sully guessed the pounding pressure from the rising flood had shifted the house enough to cause the small separation between wall and doorframe. A similar break had no doubt formed along the bottom, which was where the water had come in.

But now wasn't the time to consider structural engineering in any detail. The most relevant fact was that the walls were still too solid and the cracks far too small to allow any real give. They'd have to find another way.

He'd have to find another way.

Sully pressed his hands flat against the door, hoping to feel some sort of thudding or shaking—anything to tell him Breanna was trying to free them.

He was met with nothing but silence and stillness, nothing to instil in him any hope.

The emotional exhaustion hit him hard. He dropped his forehead against the metal, the resulting thud the only reverberation he was expecting. He knew ghosts had limited energy in the physical world, and one could only imagine how much Breanna had spent in leading Sully here, in keeping Sparrow sealed in the dry room. It was possible she had nothing left to give. Or it might be she would never be able to manipulate a door this heavy and complex into unlocking for them.

Then he heard the thud.

Solid enough he felt it against his head.

Sully pulled back from the door just enough to call out Breanna's name. He hadn't expected a verbal reply, and the one he got —while muffled and a little hard to hear—was definitely not that of a woman.

"Sully?"

Sully felt the grin spread across his face despite the situation. "Dez? What are you doing here?"

Dez's answer had him chuckling. "Figured I'd do some late-night fishing. What the hell do you think? How much water is in there?"

"Probably same as out there," Sully said. "Dez, listen. Zane Mazur—"

"Yeah, I know. Don't worry, Eva and I took care of him. He's unconscious and tied up. Eva's got him propped up against the wall at gunpoint, and I think she's just itching for an excuse. Listen, I need to get you out of there. Are the others with you?"

"Everyone's here. Bulldog, Sparrow and Paul. Everyone's okay."

"Ask Paul if there's any other way to get this door open. Mazur blew out the mechanism."

"I know. Paul said there's no other way, man."

"There has to be."

"There isn't." The grin had slipped from Sully's face as a new reality set in. He was prepared to die if he had to. He knew there was some form of a life waiting for him on the other side. But going out with Dez beside him wasn't something he was prepared to do. Dez had too much to live for, too many people who relied on him. And if Eva was here too, Kayleigh would be left an orphan if her parents didn't leave here soon. "How long until the dam gives?"

"They're going to be releasing some of it in about half-an-hour to relieve the pressure."

"How much is some?"

Silence.

"How much, Dez?"

Even muffled through a steel door, Sully could hear the reluctance in his brother's tone. "Enough to destroy The Forks."

Sully had momentarily forgotten his companions this side of the door—at least until Paul's quietly muttered, "Oh, God, no."

Dez drew Sully's attention back to the door. "Sully?"

"I'm here."

"So am I. And I'm not going anywhere. I'm going to get you out of there."

"Dez, you need to leave."

"Bullshit, I need to leave."

"You do, man. You need to leave. You and Eva have Kayleigh to worry about. I'll be fine here."

"No, Sully."

"Dez, I mean it. I'll be fine."

The response was a solid bang, louder than before, the sound of his brother's frustration. "Sully, don't you give up on me! You got that? I don't care if I have to smash through this door with my bare hands. I'm getting you out of there!"

"Dez, no. I mean it, man. Get out of here! Now!"

Dez's voice was replaced by a woman's, very clearly Eva's.

And she was pissed. "Sully, you listen to me, damn it. We are not leaving here without you. That's all there is to it."

"But Kayleigh—"

"Don't you go there. I'm her mother, and the last thing I want is to have to face her and explain how we just left you to die here. We don't give up on family, Sully. Not ever. And I'm sorry I let you down before. I was wrong, I was scared, and it's not happening again. Now, we're getting you out of there, come hell or high water."

It wasn't likely she'd meant to make a joke, but Sully took it as one anyway, letting loose a laugh that felt oddly relieving. Behind the door, he heard Eva's abashed response. "Poor choice of words."

"I love you guys," Sully said, meaning the words far more than his laughter would reflect.

The moment of levity faded fast, dying completely with Dez's next words. "Sully? It's getting weirdly cold up here. That means something, right? Something I'm not going to like?"

Sully was more excited about what that likely meant than Dez would be. "It's probably nothing."

Dez's reply was heavy with sarcasm. "As if, man. All those nights you used to crawl in with me when we were kids, this is what it felt like. It's one of them, isn't it?"

"Do you want an answer?"

"Depends. Are they here to help or make things worse?"

But Sully's attention was now on the ghosts—plural. He could sense more than Breanna. Gabriella was there, too. And someone else, someone he'd first seen at the fire at the Blakes' thirteen years ago. A teenage girl with purple hair.

None of them were visible to him, but they were all there, not bothering to manifest their energy in a visible way as they focused in on a single, possibly hopeless task.

Sully stepped closer to the door, placing one hand against it and the other on the box containing the destroyed PIN mechanism. "Use my energy," he said. "I don't care if it kills me, use all of it if it gets the others out."

He felt the draw immediately, like someone was sucking his life force out through his chest. He was struggling to keep his feet in a moment, and it was only the solid support of Bulldog's muscled arms that kept him from dropping beneath the water's surface. His hands fell from mechanism and door and, in what remained of consciousness, he could feel a heat next to him. A gently uttered curse word from Bulldog coincided with movement, the feeling of being pulled away from the heat source, and Sully opened his eyes to see an intense orange glow.

Dez's voice filtered through the gathering fog. "Jesus, Sully. The PIN pad's on fire!"

Sully heard the sounds that meant an answer to his prayers: the loud, mechanical click of the door unlocking and Dez's maniacal giggle.

A moment later, Sully was peering up at his brother's hulking presence.

"Damn it, Sull, not again," Dez muttered as he took the weight of his younger brother's drained form from Bulldog. Energy and full consciousness were on the way back, allowing Sully to follow Bulldog's movements back to the door behind which Sparrow was being kept. Paul was already there, once again unlocking the door.

"Bree, it's your brother here. I know you're trying to keep the kid safe, but you've got to leave it to me now. We need to get her out of here now, okay? The Forks is gonna go. I need you to release the door so we can get to her."

This time, when Bulldog pushed at the door, there was plenty of give—enough to send a torrent of water rushing to fill the new space. Enough to take everyone with it.

Sully felt the relentless press of water as he was sucked down below it, he and Dez taken off balance by the power of the flow. He didn't stay there long, Dez shifting quickly back to his feet and dragging Sully to the same position a moment later.

"Eva?" Dez called. "You okay?"

"All good. Mazur's going to have a headache, though."

"Bulldog?"

Sully turned his head to see their friend ploughing through the water, a small, soaked teenage girl clinging to his neck as he carried her piggyback. Bulldog was drenched and heaving breaths, but the grin he wore belied all of that.

"Never better. Paul, you coming there?"

Paul's emergence from the room was heralded by a beam of light. "Needed to find my flashlight. Let's get out of here."

They met Eva in the hall, holding a dazed-looking Mazur against the wall in an armlock. "I'm going to need a hand lugging the jerk. I think I gave him a concussion."

"We should leave the bastard here to drown," Bulldog said. "It's no more than he deserves."

"While I'm inclined to agree, he's the key to getting Danny released and the charges dropped," Eva said. "No arguments. Let's go. "

Sully's head had cleared, but Dez was staying close as the two brought up the rear in the waterlogged procession.

"How'd you find us?" Sully asked.

"You won't believe this …. Well, actually, you may be the only person who would believe it. Breanna left us her version of a trail of breadcrumbs. I had a feeling you might have come to Paul's—I mean, he said he would keep an ear to the ground for us—but at first I wasn't sure enough to risk it. Then I started seeing the iris petals."

"Really? Where?"

"Everywhere. Blowing across the bridge, floating down the streets in The Forks, sticking to the windshield. The whole way to Paul's, there they were. Would've freaked me out if I didn't have more important things to worry about."

Sully glanced around, but found no sign of Breanna's luminescent form near them. It was possible she'd expended too much energy helping to free them from the locked panic room, but he suspected otherwise; having ensured the arrival of the Dez-and-Eva cavalry, she'd been able to quietly fade away—for the time being, anyway. Whether Sully would see her again was anyone'd guess at this point.

"What I don't get is why she didn't just give us some sign the first time we came here," Dez said. "Why not show you where Sparrow was then?"

"I don't think she was worried about us finding Sparrow. Not then, anyway; she knew she was safe with Paul. What she wanted was for us to deal with the bigger threat so Sparrow would be safe once she was healthy enough to leave Paul's."

"So, mission accomplished, then."

The turning to the stairs leading to the main floor lay just ahead. Beside them stood the ghost Sully had been looking for, marking their path for Sully in case flashlights failed to show them the way. She looked the same, long hair matted and shadowing a portion of her face, hands still bound before her.

But as they neared, her head moved slowly, up and down. In Sully's mind, the movement wasn't so much agreement as approval.

As if to prove him right, she unfolded her hands, revealing not a heap of loose petals, but an entire healthy iris bloom. As the others filed blindly past her, Sully watched as the flower grew within the shelter of her fingers, becoming increasingly vibrant as it unfolded as if to catch the rays of a warm summer sun.

To Sully, the symbolism was clear enough.

"Yeah," he said. "Mission accomplished."

20

THEY MADE it across the bridge just as the dam released.

Eva had handed Zane Mazur over to the nearest patrol unit and was providing the necessary explanation when a Biblical-sized torrent came rushing from the west.

As if in irony, the rain chose that moment to stop, and Sully watched as street lights were swallowed, roadways destroyed and homes along the river's north and south banks reduced to timber, broken glass and scattered belongings.

Then The Forks was hit.

Unable to continue watching, he turned to the others standing with him. Sparrow was engulfed within Bulldog's protective embrace while Paul stood on her other side, hugging his arms across his chest as his eyes focused wide on the carnage below—or what was visible in the glow from the numerous searchlights that remained on scene. Police officers alternated between watching the devastation below and ensuring onlookers—many of them shattered Forks residents—didn't get too close to the point of danger.

Eva regained Dez's side and the two of them stood huddled together, arms encircling each other in a half-hug, eyes wide in the horror shared by everyone this side of Forks Bridge.

The expressions of pain and loss on the faces of those standing here on the South Bank proved worse than anything Sully might have seen had he been watching the flood along with everyone else. He returned his gaze below; from what he could tell, The Forks had largely disappeared beneath the dark waters of the Kimotan. And while evacuation orders had been given and received, he sensed without needing to see the grisly proof that some had decided not to leave their homes.

As it turned out, they had anyway.

Sully felt a solid arm loop around his neck and yank him into a shared hug with Dez and Eva. As expected, Dez was crying, although Sully perceived there was as much relief in his tears as sorrow.

"If you ever pull a stunt like that again, Sull, I'll kill you myself," Dez said.

Eva cupped a hand around the back of Sully's head, pulling him in until their foreheads touched. "Double for me, brother. You got that?"

Between unemployment, addictions, and now this flood, there were a lot of families who had been torn apart in Kimotan Rapids in the past few years. Sully's life wasn't perfect, never had been, but this right here—this family he'd somehow lucked into—this was as close to perfect as anyone could ever wish for.

Sully gripped Dez and Eva back hard. "I love you guys."

"We love you too," Eva said. "But that's not the answer I was looking for."

"You'll never get it out of him," Dez said. "Believe me, I've tried." Then to Sully, "Looks like you're not too old to need your big brother after all, huh?"

Sully, soaked through and chilled to the bone, felt an internal glow of warmth as he regarded the two people who'd risked their lives to save him—one of them the brother who routinely faced his own fears to protect Sully from his.

"I'm not a kid anymore, D, and I know how to handle myself," he said. "But I'll never be too old to need you."

A YEAR PASSED before Zane Mazur, snowed under by the weight of the evidence against him, pleaded guilty to the murders of Breanna Bird and Gabriella Aguado.

He had been charged with the attempted murders of Sully, Bulldog, Paul and Sparrow, but the prosecutor dropped those charges as part of the plea bargain.

"That stinks," Dez muttered next to Sully as he sat slouched on the courtroom bench. "He should have gone down for everything. He shouldn't get a walk on what he did to you."

Sully shrugged, not wanting to answer in words as one of the deputy sheriffs guarding the courtroom shot him and Dez a warning glance to be quiet. In Sully's view, it didn't matter, not really. The result was a life sentence whichever way you cut it, no parole for at least twenty years. Additional charges wouldn't affect the sentence anyway. And there was the fact Ken Barwell now knew the name of the man who'd been behind the rip-off. Paul told them Barwell had agreed to give the girl a pass (Sully expected some money had changed hands), but Zane wasn't likely to be as lucky. Sully guessed it was only a matter of time before Zane was found dead in prison under suspicious circumstances. At that point, all Sully could hope was that he didn't end up with a new ghost to deal with.

For now, what truly mattered was right here, surrounding Sully. Flynn and Mara Braddock were flanking their sons, Mara's hand gently covering Sully's. And on Mara's other side were Bulldog, Danny Newton and, between her father and uncle, a healthy-looking Iris Edwards. She'd gone into treatment within days of escaping the flood, and she and her father had become each other's primary motivation to stay clean.

Standing next to them was the other reason.

Gabriella had gone into the light shortly after Zane's arrest, but Breanna had stayed. Sully suspected, driven as she was to protect those she cared about, she wasn't going anywhere until she'd seen firsthand that justice was being done and her family left safe.

After court, once Flynn and Mara had doled out parting hugs and left, Sully and Dez joined Bulldog, Danny and Iris—as she now insisted on being called—on the courthouse steps. Iris greeted each of them with a hug while Bulldog insisted on delivering his usual playful yet firm jab to Dez's gut.

Danny smiled softly at Sully as he extended a warm hand for a shake. "I know I've said this before, but thank you. I thought I deserved to be locked up for what I put Bree through but, if you hadn't stepped in, I'd be doing another man's time and my little girl would be dead because of the same guy."

"You need to thank Breanna," Sully said. "She's the reason I kept going. She wouldn't stop, and she wouldn't let me quit either."

Danny laughed. "Yeah, sounds like Bree all right. Stubborn like a mule, that one."

"Is she here?" Iris asked.

Sully nodded to Iris's left shoulder where Breanna was standing. "Yeah. She's here."

"Is she okay?"

Sully was debating how best to answer, given that Breanna looked the same to him as when he'd first encountered her—milky-eyed, bruised and bound with that mark around her throat from where Zane had strangled her to death.

Iris cut in before Sully could come up with an answer. "I mean, I love her like she was my real mom. My real mother was a disaster. I wanted to find my dad so many times, but she told me he was dead. I didn't believe her, but I didn't know where to start looking. I ended up in Kimotan Rapids because I knew that's where I was born. But I had no one, nothing, so I ended up on the streets in less than a week. Then Bree and I found each other at The Hub, and things got a little bit better. She introduced me to Paul and they got me into some programming and into a house with other girls who were changing their lives around. After Bree died, I felt like nothing mattered anymore. I need her to be okay. If she isn't, I can't be either. Can you tell her that?"

The girl's words sparked something in Breanna that Sully hadn't ever seen besides in pictures of her: a smile. The expression proved the tipping point for a transformation that indicated she was ready to cross, the ropes falling away, the injuries fading into nothing, and her eyes clearing into shining pools of light, the fear giving way to pure love as Breanna regarded her family.

"She hears you," Sully said. "And, yeah, she's okay. She's ready to go."

Iris, already on the edge of emotion, burst into tears. "I don't want her to leave."

Sully searched his brain for the best response and was surprised when Dez provided one for him. "I know it's hard, believe me. I lost someone I love a while back in a really bad way. But I think the universe, or whatever you want to call it, looks after you. And I don't think the people we love ever really leave us. My mom always told me you've just got to learn to look for signs. That's how you'll know Breanna's still there, that she's still looking after you."

Iris sniffled and hugged her dad. "Then as long as I know she'll be all right, I will be too. Right, Dad?" She peered up at Danny, who returned her smile with his own.

"Right, my girl. Kisâkihtin, Bree. Go and find peace."

Breanna kissed each of her loved ones and gave Sully a final, lingering smile that replaced the need for words he'd never hear.

A glow formed around her, so bright and warm and full it was impossible to tell if it came from inside her or somewhere beyond, somewhere Sully didn't have the eyes to see. Into that warmth Breanna faded, an expression of the most serene peace settling over her once-anguished face.

Then she was gone.

SULLY PLACED the last couple of bottles into the beer fridge and closed the door while, a few feet away, Betty scrubbed at the stain on the bar.

"Betty?" he said. "You know Dez was kidding about putting that stain there, right? I think that's part of the wood grain."

Betty's head shifted up toward him, her gaze taking a moment to follow. "Hmm?"

"You all right?"

"Fine, Sully. Just fine. Just trying to clean this goddam stain your brother put here."

He was about to repeat his statement when Betty changed the subject. "How was court today? That bastard get what he had coming to him?"

"He pled out and got a life sentence, no parole for twenty years."

"Good. Good. And you're doing okay?"

Sully frowned. He'd known Betty a while now and although he knew she liked him well enough, she'd never before expressed much concern about him. It wasn't her style. "Yeah, I'm fine. How about you?"

She'd gone back to the stain—albeit with an expression and movements that signified her mind was elsewhere—and her eyes snapped back up at his question. "Of course I'm fine. Why wouldn't I be?"

"No reason. Just asking."

The two worked in silence as they prepared the bar for opening, and so Sully was surprised when she spoke up again.

"Something I wanted to ask you. Not sure how exactly."

Sully feigned indifference. Betty tended to get uncomfortable when someone focused on her too much. "What's up?"

He was met with another long silence, enough that he wondered whether she'd thought better of asking, until she broke it with a quietly asked question. "What do you think of your uncle?"

"Lowell?"

She looked up from her scrubbing, head tilted and eyes studying him in a way that spoke to the stupidity of Sully's query.

"He's … I don't know. He's all right, I guess."

"You don't really think that, though, do you." It was more an observation than a question, one that required a reply nonetheless.

Sully shrugged. "I've never really gotten along with him all that well, I guess. I mean, he gave me this job, so there's that. He didn't have to."

"Did you want this job?"

"I didn't really know what else I wanted to do. The only skill I really have is playing guitar, and there's not exactly a lot of call for that." He watched Betty as he considered how much he could get away with asking. Curiosity won out. "Why do you want to know about Lowell?"

"No reason," she said. "Just wondering. That's all."

It wasn't all. Far from it, if Sully was any judge of people. But whatever Betty had been wanting to ask, possibly to reveal, had slipped irretrievably back into her mind, far out of his immediate reach.

For now, the two of them worked in his uncle's bar within a silence that had become more companionable. And then, as his eyes caught slight movement at his left side, he realized two had become three.

The spirit formed slowly, like a soft morning mist caught in a gentle breeze as it drifted across a dewy lawn. The first thing he saw was a wet tuft of red hair not far above the level of his waist, followed by a shining set of green eyes. Although the ghost was still materializing, Sully didn't need to see the additional features to recognize the child. He'd seen him before, long ago, standing next to the creek that ran behind the house where Sully had been lucky enough to do most of his growing up. He recognized the boy from photographs, and from the colouring he shared with his father and now-grown big brother.

Sully stared down into the child's eyes, wide with unspoken meaning, with the message he'd never been able to impart.

"Aiden?"

So fixed was he on the small face that Sully temporarily forgot where he was. A question from Betty brought him back, had his gaze snapping from Aiden to his boss. "Did you say something, Sully?"

Sully looked back down to his side. Aiden, whose little body had been pulled from the water sixteen years ago, was gone.

There was no sign of him, nothing to tell Sully why he'd come here, what he needed.

No proof he'd ever been here at all.

"Sorry," Sully said. "I thought I saw something."

"What?"

"Nothing," Sully said.

"That happen to you a lot?"

Sully ran a hand along the bar's smooth surface, wishing he had a stain of his own to focus on. Anything to distract him from her question, that sudden vision of Aiden, of the unseen world that constantly encroached on the life he'd struggled so hard to build for himself.

He offered her as much truth as he could.

"Yeah," he said. "All the time."

ABOUT THE AUTHOR

Fascinated by ghost stories and crime fiction, H.P. has been writing both for well over two decades, drawing on more than fifteen years in a career in a criminal justice setting. Raised on a farm on the Canadian Prairies, H.P. enjoys reading, portrait drawing, travel and spending time with family and friends.